"There's a lot of bad blood between our families."

A smile bloomed on his face and he rolled to his back. Emma smoothed her hand over his firm chest. "I knew you were a good guy, Daniel. That's why I wanted so badly to be able to prove you wrong. I think it's time for us to turn our backs on this feud between Stones and Edens."

"Is there an opt-out form I missed?"

She playfully swatted his arm and leaned down to kiss him softly. "No. I'm just saying that we can say that we won't play those sorts of games. We're the newest generation of both businesses, right? I want to find a way to get past the negativity. I don't see the point in it."

A deep crease formed between his eyes. He seemed leery at best. "Have any ideas how to do that?"

* * *

A Cinderella Seduction is part of the Lone Star Empire series.

Dear Reader,

Thanks for picking up *A Cinderella Seduction*! It's the *second Eden Empire* book about the heiresses of the Eden family who are running their grandmother's Manhattan department store.

This book centers on Emma, the half sister neither Sophie nor Mindy knew about until the reading of Grandma Eden's will in *A Christmas Temptation*. Emma is truly a modern-day Cinderella, raised with very little until she inherits a fortune and two sisters and is thrust into a glamorous world of money and high fashion. Emma has always been quiet and shy, but she's forced to take center stage when the New York tabloids become infatuated with beguiling her and dub her a princess. It's all for the sake of Eden's department store.

Enter our "prince," Daniel Stone, a Brit in the United States opening a New York location of his family's department store, Stone's. The only members of the Eden family Daniel knows of are Sophie and her sister Mindy. So when he meets Emma at a fashion show, he has no idea she's part and parcel of his family's biggest competitors. That night, they flirt wildly and start to fall hard, and then a broken zipper puts them in close quarters and Daniel's suit jacket becomes the glass slipper. Once Emma returns it and identities are revealed, they're left to grapple with a decades-old family feud between the Stones and the Edens. There are twists and turns right up until the very end, when love must save the day.

I hope you enjoy this Harlequin Desire—style retelling of Cinderella! Drop me a line any time at karen@karen booth.net. I love hearing from readers! And don't miss the next Eden Empire book, *A Bet with Benefits*!

Karen

KAREN BOOTH

A CINDERELLA SEDUCTION

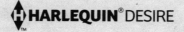

ISBN-13: 978-1-335-60377-7

A Cinderella Seduction

Copyright © 2019 by Karen Booth

HARLEQUIN®
www.Harlequin.com

Printed in U.S.A.

Karen Booth is a Midwestern girl transplanted in the South, raised on '80s music and repeated readings of *Forever* by Judy Blume. When she takes a break from the art of romance, she's listening to music with her nearly grown kids or sweet-talking her husband into making her a cocktail. Learn more about Karen at karenbooth.net.

Books by Karen Booth

Harlequin Desire

The Best Man's Baby
The Ten-Day Baby Takeover
Snowed in with a Billionaire

The Eden Empire

A Christmas Temptation
A Cinderella Seduction

Dynasties: Secrets of the A-List

Tempted by Scandal

Visit her Author Profile page at Harlequin.com, or karenbooth.net, for more titles.

You can find Karen Booth on Facebook, along with other Harlequin Desire authors, at Facebook.com/harlequindesireauthors!

For Piper Trace. Every book I write has your delightfully crazy fingerprints all over it.

One

The room was pitch-black and perfectly still, except for the ring of Daniel Stone's cell phone. He rolled over in bed and blindly slapped his hand on the nightstand, fumbling for the device. He didn't bother checking the caller ID. Despite the five-hour time difference between London and New York, his mother never worried she might be calling too early.

"It's 5:49 in the bloody a.m.," he croaked, pushing himself up in bed. He switched on the lamp. The bright light shot across his room, and he squinted hard until his eyes adjusted. "What could possibly be so important?" The second of April, it was still dark out. His three dogs, Mandy, Buck and Jolly, were asleep at the foot of the bed.

"Are you going to see spaces for the new store today?"

His mother always jumped straight into business. She'd been this way as long as he could remember, but ever since his brother, William, had passed away, it was even more impossible to keep her content.

"I meet the real estate agent at nine. Two spaces to see today. I'm hopeful." That was a lie. Daniel was anything but optimistic, but he had to keep up the charade. It had been his idea to forge ahead with his mother's long-held dream of a New York location of Stone's, the family's wildly successful department store chain based in the UK. He'd hoped it might finally make her happy. So far, it was doing nothing but making Daniel second-guess himself. He'd been in Manhattan for three weeks now and he'd only come up empty-handed.

"You'll ring me when you've had your look?" she asked.

"Don't I always check in?" Daniel hated that she still had so little faith in him. He'd worked for the family his entire adult life. Then again, he'd spent those years playing second chair to his brother. That changed a year ago, when William's black Aston Martin hit a slick of oil on a road outside London and went careening off a bridge. The Stone family was no stranger to tragedy, but this one had hit especially hard.

Daniel's father now spent his days and a considerable chunk of the family fortune sailing the world. No boat was fast enough, no stretch of ocean too dangerous. He was currently somewhere off the coast of West Africa. His mother despised her husband's new hobby and had become equally reckless with the family business. Daniel felt as though he was babysitting them both, an unfair situation given that they still felt he needed to prove his worth.

"I trust you're prepared for the Empire State fashion show this evening?" she asked.

His mother was the micromanaging sort of boss. Never mind that he was thirty-four and this had become wearisome. "I am."

"Taking a date?"

"I've been busy." Daniel was not in New York to make friends. He certainly was not in America for romance. Women only made life complicated. No, he was here to prove to his parents that he had things well in hand and it was time for them both to retire. William might have been the golden boy, but Daniel refused to be the black sheep because of the argument he and his brother had had the night of the accident.

"I'll take that as a no then. Now, please tell me you remember your marching orders for this evening."

"I track down Nora Bradford and convince her to design a line exclusive to Stone's."

"I can't emphasize enough how important this is. Eden's has not done right by her and her designs. She's too talented to be selling an entire line of her gorgeous garments in a second-rate department store."

Daniel choked back a grumble. He hadn't realized his mother still had an ax to grind with Eden's until he'd already begun his initiative of opening Stone's New York. If he'd know this much, he never would've suggested it. "It's not second-rate. I've seen it."

"You're wrong. And you know how much I despised Victoria Eden. The woman was vindictive."

Victoria Eden, the founder of Eden's, had given his mother her start in retail years ago, grooming her to be the manager of the Eden's flagship store in Manhattan. Eden's had locations all over the world, and Stone's, a business founded by his grandparents, was dying on the vine. His mother had been sent to New York to learn the secrets of Eden's. But when Victoria found out, she not only fired his mother, she got even with his family by convincing suppliers to stop selling to Stone's. It nearly crippled their company. A family feud was born.

"I'm aware."

"Our move into New York has everything to do with destroying Eden's. It does make me sad, though, that William isn't here to be a part of it."

Daniel slumped down in bed. Jolly, the English bulldog that had belonged to his brother, crawled her way closer, curling up at his hip. Daniel gave her a scratch behind the ear, but she growled. She wasn't always affectionate with him. Even Jolly thought he didn't quite measure up to William. "Our best strategy is to focus on being Stone's. May the strongest survive," he said.

"The Eden sisters are no competition. Those three know nothing about running a department store. One of them has been off in the south of France her entire life, doing nothing."

Daniel closed his eyes and pinched the bridge of his nose. "I need to take the dogs out. I'll ring you later."

Daniel said goodbye and shuffled into the kitchen to put on some tea. With the kettle heating up, he strode into the living room. Through the tall windows, he watched the sun begin to creep up over the horizon, illuminating the edges of the lush green tree line of Central Park, tucked neatly inside the hard city landscape. This was a million-dollar view, the sort of vista most people only dreamed of.

Still, something was missing. He probably felt that way because it wasn't London. There was nothing tying him to this luxury high-rise or this impossibly busy metropolis. The sooner he found a location for Stone's, got the store opened and staffed, the sooner he could head back to England and whatever future he could manage to build.

For the fifth time in as many days, Emma Stewart stared into the mirror, scrutinizing herself and her attire. Was this dress chic enough for the Empire State fashion show tonight? It was flattering. Tasteful and tailored. The gray midweight crepe fabric had a beautiful drape. Plus, she had on somewhat daring shoes—black Manolo Blahnik pumps that her half sister Sophie had instructed her to buy. The ensemble was befitting a woman with an executive position at Eden's department store. But would it make the cut in a room full of designers, celebrities, fashion editors and models? That, she did not know.

Emma took a final skeptical turn in front of the mirror, gathered her long brown hair and reached back to unzip the dress. It was just going to have to do. The fact of the matter was she was comfortable wearing gray. She might someday be a bolder, sexier version of Emma Stewart, but not today. She wasn't ready. It didn't matter that she now had a net worth of over a billion dollars, owned a swank apartment overlooking Central Park, and was CFO of the largest department store in the city. Three months ago, Emma's checking account held thirty-four bucks, she was renting a tired one-bedroom apartment in New Jersey, had a fleet-footed brown mouse for an uninvited roommate, and was a junior CPA at a tiny accounting firm. She wouldn't be at ease in a dress that might make her the center of attention, mostly because she'd never been the center of anything.

She tucked the dress inside a garment bag in order to take it to work. She and her half sisters, Mindy and Sophie, were not only attending Empire State, they were going to get ready together, at Eden's. Sophie had arranged for a hair stylist and makeup artist, which was perfect, since Emma had time for neither this morning. She was going to be late if she didn't get out the door. Putting her hair up in a ponytail, she bothered only with sunscreen, a light coat of mascara and lip balm, and dressed in her usual work attire— black trousers and a silk blouse. To mix things up, the blouse was royal-blue. She also decided to stick with the sky-high pumps she planned to wear that night. Twice daring counted for something, right?

Out in the hall, she waited for the elevator, mentally running through the workday ahead. She'd been at Eden's for three months now, and the days weren't getting any easier. It was a bizarre situation to begin with—in late December, Emma had been called to the reading of Victoria Eden's will. Emma had known Victoria Eden only as her cousins' grandmother, and the owner of Eden's, the largest department store in the city. Turned out that Victoria Eden was also Emma's grandma. Emma's mom had had an affair twenty-seven years ago with her sister's husband. Everyone kept it a secret, especially from Emma. But Victoria Eden blew the top off this powder keg when she left one-third of her empire to the third granddaughter nobody knew about—Emma. The other two-thirds of the store went to Sophie and Mindy Eden, women Emma had always believed were her cousins. In truth, they were her half sisters. Emma still wasn't sure what to make of that. She'd grown up an only child. She'd always wanted siblings, but this was a lot to grapple with at once.

Finally, the elevator dinged. Emma glanced down at her pumps as the door slid open, but then her sights landed on someone else's shoes. A man's shiny black wingtips to be exact, leading to charcoal dress pants on ridiculously long legs. The hem of a suit coat led to a trim waist, under which was a crisp white shirt over a broad chest and shoulders, all topped off with a tousled head of thick brown hair swept back from the forehead of a man she'd never before had the good fortune to run into.

Icy blue eyes connected with hers. The man didn't say a word. He merely cleared his throat and pressed his hand against the elevator door as it threatened to close.

Emma hopped on board while a flush of heat washed over her. "I'm sorry. Morning. On my way to work. Too much on my mind." She added a casual laugh for good measure.

The towering man said nothing in response, folding his hands in front of him and staring straight ahead at the doors.

"Are you on your way to work, too?" she asked.

The man glanced over at her and nodded. "Yes."

Ooh. A British accent. "Have you lived in the building long?" She'd been in the building for nearly two months now and had made friends with almost none of her neighbors. Not that she hadn't tried. She brought pumpkin muffins to the couple who moved in down the hall from her. They seemed…bemused. Emma realized her tragic mistake as soon as the wife said, "How sweet. Homemade and everything." She should have brought something from Dean & Deluca or Zabar's at the very least. Next time, it'd be chocolate truffles and a bottle of champagne. Emma was capable of faking her way through this world if she simply put a little thought into it.

The man shook his head. "No." He raked his fingers through his hair.

Emma had another four or five questions queued

up in her head, one of which was whether she could smell him some more. His cologne was intriguing—warm and woodsy. Unfortunately, the doors slid open and he stepped aside. "Please," he said. If he was that good with single-syllable words, Emma could only imagine what might happen to her if he chose to utter an entire sentence in her presence.

Emma scurried off the elevator to the right and the main lobby, but the British mystery man strode left through the entrance to the parking garage. She looked longingly as he disappeared from view. Maybe she could get her driver to meet her in there next time. She might be missing out on a whole slew of handsome men.

Or perhaps she should just get to work and stop thinking about handsome men. Eden's was her entire future, one she'd never dreamed she could have. There was no room for distractions now.

After twenty minutes of stop-and-go Manhattan rush-hour traffic, Emma's driver dropped her at Eden's. Lizzie, the receptionist in the administrative offices, hardly let her step off the elevator before speaking. "Mindy and Sophie are waiting for you in Sophie's office. They want to talk about Empire State."

Emma forced a smile. "Thanks. I'll head in." Simply hearing the name of the big charity fashion show made her nervous again. Their grandmother had apparently attended the event every year. Tonight would be the debut of the three sisters, Mindy, Sophie and Emma, as the new faces of Eden's department store.

"Emma. Good morning." Sophie sprang up from her desk, swung her long, strawberry blond hair over her shoulder and gave Emma a hug. She was wearing a gorgeous navy blue dress and killer red heels. Sophie was the epitome of put-together, and quite frankly, everything Emma hoped to be someday.

"Hey, Em," Mindy offered, unsubtly eyeing Emma from head to toe. Mindy was wearing a plum-colored pencil skirt and short peplum jacket. She didn't have a wardrobe as funky as Sophie, but she always looked impeccable. "I see we went with black pants again."

"I was in a rush. I just grabbed what I knew would look good." Emma stood next to Sophie's desk rather than sitting. She didn't want to be here for long.

"Is that your dress for tonight?" Mindy asked, pointing to the garment bag Emma was still toting.

"Oh. Uh. Yes."

"Sophie and I would like to see it, please. No more keeping it a secret."

Emma walked over to Sophie's coat tree and hung up the dress, unzipping it from its bag. She pressed her lips together tightly, preparing herself for what these two might say. Anything was fair game. They worked in an industry built on first impressions and style, and she wasn't doing great on either front. But, and this was a big but, Sophie and Mindy had grown up in a household where money was never an issue, where they were encouraged to dress in any way they saw fit. Emma, however, had grown up buying her clothes at discount stores, and had been preached the value of blending in.

"Well?" Emma stood a little straighter, holding the dress up and steeling herself for the onslaught.

"No way," Mindy said. "It's terrible."

Sophie shot Mindy a look and got up from her desk again, rushing over to where Emma was standing. "Oh, I don't know. Gray is a hot color this season." She took the hem of the dress in her hand. "I think the problem is that this isn't really an evening dress. And it's not very fun. This is a fun night. It's a night for standing out."

Emma had been afraid of that. "It's not my fault that I'm not up to speed on the fashion world. Up until three months ago, I was working in an accountant's office and had no money."

"You know you can't tell anyone about that," Sophie said, holding her finger to her lips.

Oh, right. The family fable. Soon after Emma's inheritance was announced, Mindy and Sophie had concocted a story to explain Emma's absence from the public lives of the Eden family. They owned up to the poor behavior of their father, but not the fact that the truth had been hidden from Emma for her entire life and she'd lived with very little money. They felt it might reflect badly on their grandmother, and in turn, the store. Emma was to tell everyone that she'd spent her formative years with a private tutor in France, then moved back to the States to quietly pursue her education in finance. It wasn't that far from the truth, except that she'd lived in New Jersey and been home-schooled. Emma would have fought the lie, but it made it easier to exist in this world of money and power. It was a shred of a pedigree, and she'd take what she could get.

"Don't worry. I won't say anything."

"Anyway, that dress is a snooze fest. You need to find something else." Mindy crossed her legs and bobbed her foot impatiently.

"I'll go down to jewelry and find a necklace to brighten it up," Emma said.

Sophie scrunched up her face. "I'm not sure that will be enough."

Emma wasn't going to stand here and endure their criticism. She did not want to appear weak or foolish in front of her half sisters. She still wasn't sure they had her best interests in mind. "I'll pick out a different dress then. Surely we have something in the store that will work." Head held high, Emma marched out into the hall, but she felt anything but confident. There was too much sheer embarrassment coursing through her veins.

She darted into the safety of her office and flipped on the light. This had been her grandmother's office when she was still alive. Every time Emma walked into this room, she was reminded of what might have been. What if the family secret had come out when she was a little girl? She would have had a chance to know her grandmother. She might have known her father. She might have been a completely different person, the sort of woman who had no problem picking the right dress for an event like tonight. But no, all of that had slipped between Emma's fingers and she hadn't even known it was there.

Sophie appeared in the office doorway. "May I come in?"

"I don't want to turn this into a big thing, okay? I'll figure it out." Emma sought the comfort of the chair behind her desk, putting a big piece of furniture between herself and her half sister.

"I know that. But why don't you let me come with you?"

"I'm a grown woman. I can pick out my clothes." Emma didn't want to sound defensive. The truth was that she needed help. She at least needed someone to tell her she didn't look ridiculous.

Sophie took a seat in an available chair. "You know, the first time our grandmother took me to this event, I was a wreck. I had no clue what to wear. I really needed Gram to point me in the right direction."

"Well, she's not around to help me, is she?" Emma hated that tone in her voice, but it came from a very deep place. She'd been robbed of the relationship with her family.

"She's not. And I'm sorry about that. But I'd like to help. I've been to this event four times now. I can help you find the perfect dress."

Emma didn't want to admit it, but this was what she'd been waiting for—the smallest of opportunities. A door opened. Plus, the clock was ticking. "I don't know when I'll have time. My schedule is hell, and I hate doing things at the last minute. I'm a planner. I don't like surprises."

Sophie stood. "Don't worry about that. I need to run down to the designer department this morning, anyway. I'll find a few things and you can pick from those. Sound good?"

"Just don't go too overboard, okay? I'm not a showy person."

"You don't have to be showy to be a showstopper." Sophie looked at her phone, which she always had in hand. "Meet me in the private fitting room in two hours."

Emma didn't have a great feeling about this, but what choice did she have? She couldn't go to this event looking as if she didn't belong. She desperately wanted to stop being the proverbial fish out of water. "I'll be there."

Two

After a morning of crunching numbers, Emma found herself with Sophie in the private fitting room reserved for Eden's most important customers. Emma had never tried clothes on in such a lavish setting. The room not only had a lovely sitting area with elegant upholstered slipper chairs in silvery velvet, it had especially flattering lighting, and came with a valet who took drink orders. For Eden's wealthiest and most influential clients, this was their shopping experience—an oasis tucked away in a quiet corner of an otherwise bustling department store.

The valet appeared with two flutes of champagne.

"Really?" Emma asked, when Sophie offered her a glass. "It's the middle of the day."

"I'm hoping we'll have a reason to toast and celebrate. I wanted to ask if you'll be one of my brides-maids."

Emma could hardly believe what she was hear-ing. "Really?" As soon as she'd said it, she realized how inappropriate and knee-jerk her response was. If she didn't want to feel like an outsider in this fam-ily, she had to stop assuming that role. "I mean, yes. Of course. I would love it. Such an honor."

Sophie grinned and held out her glass. Emma clinked it with hers. "Perfect. I still need to figure out who's designing the dresses, but I'll let you know."

Emma was in a state of delight and shock. Custom designed bridesmaids' dresses? "Sounds wonderful."

Sophie sank down onto one of the chairs, her skirt billowing in a poof. "It's funny, but I think of Gram every time I drink champagne."

"What was she like?" Emma sat in the chair op-posite and took a small sip. It was so delicious. The bubbles tickled her nose.

"Gram was amazing. My idol, really. I loved her to pieces. But she rubbed some people the wrong way. She could be a ruthless businesswoman."

Emma pushed back any sadness over not having known her grandmother. "All women have to be ruth-less at some point, don't they?"

Sophie eagerly nodded. "If they want to be a suc-cess, yes."

"Speaking of which, I happened to notice that our exclusive arrangement with Nora Bradford still hasn't been renewed."

Sophie frowned. "I know. They're dragging their

feet. You know, we lost two of our exclusive design-ers in late December, right before you started. If we lose Nora, it would be devastating."

"Why do you think this is happening?"

"People aren't treating us the way they did when Gram was in charge."

Emma took another sip. "Sounds like we need to get a few things in line."

"I'm working on it. I'll need your help at some point. For now, I'm hoping the dress I picked for to-night might help. It's in the fitting room."

"Dress? Singular?"

"I know I said I'd give you some choices, but this one is perfect. It just came in this morning. It's one of our Nora Bradford exclusives." Sophie shooed her into the fitting room. "Go on. Go look."

Emma ducked inside the dressing area. On the hook was a dress she wouldn't have dared to choose. Ice blue, strapless and sparkly and daring. It was so far outside her comfort zone it was in a different zip code. And maybe that was exactly what she needed.

Wasting no time, she shed her work clothes and slipped into the garment. "Can you help with the zip-per?" she called.

Sophie poked her head inside and her face lit up. "That's it. That's the dress. It's even better than I imagined. Now suck in your breath."

With a quick zip, Emma was squeezed in. She looked down at herself. "I don't know. I've never worn a strapless dress before and there's all this fabric." She fussed with the strips of pale blue organza that made up the skirt. If she stood still, her legs were hidden, but the second she moved, the strips swished open like streamers in the breeze. "What if I trip? And I can barely breathe." The bodice was holding her tight, all the way down to her hips.

"Oh, there is no breathing in a strapless dress. Not if you want it to stay up all night. And really, you look incredible. It's perfect for your body. You look sexy and glamorous."

"I do?" If it wasn't for the freckles on her cheeks and the earrings she wore every day, Emma wouldn't have even known it was her.

"Yes. And the best part is I've instructed the department manager to keep the rest of the inventory off the showroom floor until tomorrow morning. You'll be the only one at Empire State wearing this."

Emma studied herself in the mirror, dropping her head to the side and swishing the skirt. The dress looked like magic. Maybe this really was the right choice. "Okay. This is the one."

Sophie grinned with pride and clapped her hands on Emma's shoulders. "I don't want you to be nervous about tonight. You'll be amazing. And I'll be there the whole time, okay?"

Emma felt so much better than she had that morning. "Thank you for helping me. And thank you for asking me to be a bridesmaid. That means a lot to me."

"Of course. You're my sister. It only seems right that you'd be a part of my wedding."

Emma had never felt so optimistic. Sophie was

making such an effort to include her. Emma was starting to feel like a real part of the Eden clan, less like
a person who was unwittingly plopped down in the
middle of it. She would get what she'd missed out on
during her twenty-seven years in the world—a close
relationship with siblings, the camaraderie of an ex-
tended family. She felt sure of it now.

From the bench in the corner, Emma's phone
buzzed. "Oh, shoot. I have a call." Back to reality.

"I'll help you out of the dress. Then I need to get
Lizzie to order me some lunch."

Emma changed and raced upstairs. One of Eden's
personal shoppers steamed the gown and delivered
it to her office, along with a pair of strappy silver
Blahniks Sophie had picked out. The dress was the
only thing Emma looked at as she finished up her call.
The fabric, the style, the price tag—it all seemed un-
real, as if it wasn't meant for her.

Mindy appeared in Emma's office doorway around
three. "The hair and makeup people are here, but we
have a problem. Sophie's sick."

"Is she okay?"

Mindy shook her head. "A stomach bug or something she ate. I sent her home. I don't see any way she
can come tonight. Looks like it's just you and me."

Great. The sister who hates me. Emma felt queasy
herself. Her security blanket was gone. "Oh. Okay."

"We need to leave right at five or we'll get stuck
in traffic forever. I'll send in the hair and makeup
people."

Emma was now not only nervous, she was dreading tonight. Before she had time to think about it, a man and a woman invaded her office with brushes, hair clips, a curling iron, and every shade of lipstick and type of hair product you could imagine. They wheeled her across her office in her chair and parked her in front of a full-length mirror they'd brought.

The male stylist took her hair out of the ponytail and tutted. "I'm Anthony. This is going to take a while."

The makeup artist at least offered a smile. "I'm Charity. It's going to take me some time, too."

"Oh. Okay. Well, I'm Emma."

"We know," they answered in unison.

Charity dug through a case of makeup, picking up tubes and examining the colors. "I'm going to cover your freckles, if that's okay." She pointed to Emma's cheeks.

"I like them."

Charity shook her head. "I don't think they'll photograph well. There will be paparazzi tonight. You want to look good."

Emma hadn't taken the time to think about the fate of her freckles, and definitely not photographers. "Do whatever you need to do."

The duo went to work, tugging and dabbing, prodding and pulling, spraying and spritzing. Emma kept her eyes closed whenever possible. They were doing too many things that she would never do to herself.

"Voilà," Anthony said a good forty-five minutes later. He was like Michelangelo presenting a masterpiece.

Emma opened her eyes and blinked several times. If it wasn't for the same clothes she'd worn to work, she never would have known it was her. Her hair was tugged back in a dramatic updo, she had long false lashes and smoky eyes. She looked fantastic, practically ready for the cover of a magazine. So this was what it was like to be glamorous.

"Wow," was all she could say.

"Emma, you are a stunning woman if you put some work into it," Charity said.

Perhaps that was her problem. She hadn't been trying hard enough. "Thank you so much. Both of you."

"Call us anytime."

Not wanting Mindy to be angry with her, Emma closed and locked her office door and dressed. She called in Lizzie to help with the zipper.

"You are so lucky," Lizzie said, looking at Emma with eyes full of wistful envy. It was a bizarre feeling. Emma and Lizzie were more alike than she and Sophie or Mindy.

"Maybe we can figure out a way for you to come with us next year."

"Really?"

Emma nodded. "In fact, I promise to do whatever I can to make it happen, okay?"

Lizzie grinned from ear to ear. "Wow. Something to look forward to."

Mindy walked in wearing a supershort magenta dress with a plunging neckline and sky-high Christian Louboutins with the signature red bottoms. She surveyed Emma's new look. "They did wonders. You hardly look like yourself at all."

Gee, thanks. "You look great, too."

Lizzie rushed out of the room when the reception phone started to ring.

"Hey, so, I need a favor from you tonight," Mindy said, digging through one of her prized Hermès clutches. "I have a friend meeting me there, so I won't be able to spend much time with you. But I don't want you to tell Sophie."

"Does this friend happen to be the guy that Sophie doesn't like?"

Mindy pursed her lips. "His name is Sam, okay? He's in town for a few days and I really want to see him. And yes, Sophie hates him. But that's her problem, not mine. It has something to do with her fiancé, Jake."

Emma was tempted to ask what was in it for her to keep the secret but decided against it. She needed to forge a connection with Mindy, somehow. "Okay. My lips are zipped."

"Awesome. I owe you one."

Well, that was something. "No problem."

Mindy's phone beeped with a text. "My driver's here."

Downstairs, they climbed into the back of a black stretch SUV. As they whizzed through the city, Emma tried to ignore her nerves. She tried to ignore that little voice inside her head that said that every last person at this event was going to know she didn't belong. There was only so much refinement she could fake.

What if someone asked her where she went to school and she forgot the canned story Sophie and Mindy had cooked up about private school in France? What if someone asked about her family and she accidentally blurted the truth, that until three months ago, she was the deep dark family secret? Even worse, what if no one asked her anything at all?

As the driver pulled into the line of limousines and black town cars, Emma could see the paparazzi's camera flashes popping like crazy. *The red carpet.* Emma's stomach wobbled. She wasn't practiced in the art of posing for cameras. She didn't know how to hold her head at the right angle or slant her leg to make herself look skinny, or even how to properly plant her hand on her hip. This could be a disaster.

"Anything I need to know about this first part?" she asked Mindy.

Her half sister eyed herself in a compact mirror, them clamped it shut. "Follow my lead. You'll be fine."

Mindy climbed out of the car first and Emma followed. A woman with a clipboard was checking names, but she took one glance at Mindy and knew exactly who she was. "Mindy Eden. Nice to see you. Who do you have with you tonight?" the woman asked, her tone syrupy.

"My sister Emma."

A deep crease formed between the woman's eyes. "I thought your sister was Sophie."

"Long story," was all Mindy said, patting the woman on the shoulder and waving Emma ahead.

Emma stepped onto the red carpet, her heart thundering in her chest. She followed every move Mindy made, mimicking her stance and posture, every elegant quality Emma did not possess naturally. The paparazzi were quite taken with the couple in front of them, but then a few spotted Mindy and she quickly became their focus.

"Mindy! Over here!"

"This way, Mindy!"

Emma didn't know what to do, so she hung back, letting the photographers focus on her sister. Mindy smiled effortlessly, turning her head just so, shaking her shiny red tresses with all the confidence in the world. She was such a pro. Emma felt like a kid standing on the edge of the pool with water wings.

"Who's with you tonight?" a photographer asked.

Mindy cast her sights at Emma. Emma worried that Mindy might throw her under the bus and pretend she didn't know her.

"My youngest sister, Emma, of course." She reached for her hand, and before Emma knew what was happening, a million flashbulbs went off as she stood next to Mindy. These strangers were taking her picture and saying her name.

Emma! Emma!

Mindy stepped back and left Emma at center stage. She smiled, willing her face to be relaxed and natural. She planted her hand on her hip in what she hoped was the appropriate place.

Why are we just meeting you now, Emma?

She hadn't prepared for questions. "I've been living in France. Just came back to the States to help my sisters run Eden's."

Who are you wearing?

"Nora Bradford, of course. The gown is an Eden's exclusive. It'll be available in the store starting tomorrow." She glanced down for an instant and knew that if she didn't move, they'd miss the most dramatic part of the design. Hands on her hips, she turned in a circle, the skirt flying up and showing off her legs. She was nearly blinded by flashbulbs when she'd completed the three-sixty.

"Let's get out of here," Mindy mumbled in her ear.

"Did I make a mistake?" Emma asked nervously.

"It was fine. You just can't give them too much."

She and Mindy strolled the remaining length of the red carpet and stepped into a lavish room already packed with people. Emma's eyes were still adjusting from the bright lights of the cameras to the moodier party atmosphere, but she could see enough to know that beauty was everywhere.

Mindy tapped Emma on the shoulder. "Sam's here." She waved across the room, and sure enough, a tall and handsome man with jet-black hair waved back. "I'll see you later."

"Wait," Emma blurted. "Will I see you at our seats?"

Mindy was distracted by her quickly approaching guy. "I'll be with Sam. Not sure where I'll see you. My driver will take you home. You have his number?"

Emma nodded. Mindy's driver had taken her all over the city before she had a driver of her own. "I do."

Just like that, Mindy was gone. Emma turned to the crowd, unsure what to do. She disliked being by herself. If Sophie had been able to come, Emma still would have been the person nobody knew, but at least she wouldn't have been alone. In this big room filled with fabulous people, she felt insignificant. Like a speck of dust floating around everyone's head, unnoticed.

A waiter walked by with a tray topped with glasses of champagne. Emma snagged one and took a long sip. Then another. She scanned the room, and for an instant, she wondered if she'd already had too much to drink. Either that or an optical illusion was walking into the room. Her heart nearly stopped beating. It was Mr. Brit from her building. Sure, he'd been less than friendly in the elevator, but she was now officially intrigued. His accent alone had been enough to interest her, but was he somehow involved in fashion? Perhaps a wealthy investor? Hopefully, he wasn't one of those men who habitually dated models.

She studied him as inconspicuously as possible, sucking down the last of her champagne. Damn, he looked good in a tux. Ridiculously good. Like it had been sewn around his broad shoulders. His light brown hair was a bit of a tousled mess, but she liked that about him. It made him seem human. Everything else about him was a little too perfect—the five o'clock shadow, the kissable lips, the way he could see over the top of nearly everyone in the crowd. For a moment, she imagined herself combing her fingers through his bed-head hair and allowing her hands to get completely lost.

But the best thing about Mr. Brit was that he seemed to be alone. Just like her. Did she have the nerve to approach him? They did have a slight rapport. There was at least a starting point for a conversation. And she still had the questions she'd cooked up in the elevator. She could likely hold her own for a good ten minutes.

As if he sensed she was watching him, he turned his head. Their gazes connected. Emma would've looked away if he didn't have her so locked in. His eyes were like a tractor beam designed to pull her across the room. And maybe that was precisely what she needed to do.

Three

If Daniel wasn't mistaken, he hadn't merely laid eyes on one of the most beautiful women he'd ever seen, she was coming his way. He never played coy, so he made eye contact again, but still his pulse raced. She was stunning—floating through the room as if her feet never touched the floor. Her dark hair was swept up and back from her face, accentuating her graceful neck. He hadn't pondered kissing a woman in that region for months. Now it was all he could think about.

"Hello." She had an air of self-assurance that was simply breathtaking. This was a woman who was accustomed to taking what she wanted.

"Hello yourself."

"We've got to stop meeting like this."

Taken by surprise, he couldn't help but laugh.

What a confident way to greet a stranger. "Clever."
He held out his hand. "I'm Daniel." He stopped short
of offering his last name. No one knew he was in New
York scouting locations for Stone's, and he intended
to keep it that way. Luckily, few people in the States
knew him by sight. In London, it would be a different matter.

She slid her long, delicate fingers against his and
shook his hand, sending ripples of warmth through
him. "Emma." She let go, leaving his palm tingling.

"So, tell me, Emma, what brings you to an event
like this?"

She looked up at him from beneath a fringe of
dark lashes that brought out the sheer sexiness of her
brown eyes. "My job. I work for Eden's."

A waiter walked by with champagne, which gave
Daniel a moment to decide how best to proceed. This
gorgeous woman who'd managed to find him was
employed by the company his mother considered the
enemy. "Can I interest you in a drink?"

"Yes, please."

Daniel took two flutes and handed one to Emma.
"To new friends?"

Emma shook her head. "You can't toast with a
question. To new friends." She clinked her glass with
his.

For the first time in three weeks, Daniel wasn't so
eager to get home to London. He also found himself
dismissing his commitment to staying away from the
fairer sex. "Hear, hear." He took a sip, studying her

rosy-pink lips as they curved around the glass. "What do you do for Eden's?"

"Number crunching, mostly."

The lights in the room flashed off and on. Emma looked up, then returned her sights to him. "I guess we have to find out seats?" The crowd began moving toward the double doors leading into the adjoining room.

Something in Daniel's gut told him he was an idiot if he let Emma get away. They were just getting started. "Did you come alone?"

"I didn't, but my date ditched me."

"Date?"

"My sister. I mean my half sister. It's complicated."

"I see. Well, if I'm not being too forward, where are you sitting?" he asked.

A sheepish smile crossed her lips. "My seats are in the front row. I have an extra if you want to join me. My other sister wasn't able to make it."

"I'm sorry to hear about your sister." But he wasn't sorry he would be sitting with Emma. "And I'd love to join you." He didn't have to tell her that his seat was also in the front row. He'd let her think she was giving him a thrill.

They made their way inside and found their seats along the runway. Daniel subtly surveyed the rest of the front-row attendees, and spotted Nora Bradford, the designer he had to speak with before the end of the evening. He'd have to find a time to break away from Emma, which was a real shame, but for now, he would enjoy himself.

"You haven't told me what you do, Daniel," Emma said.

He couldn't afford to tell her the truth. He had no idea of her stature at Eden's or to whom she might end up speaking. "I'm here in the city looking at some real estate for my family's business." Not a lie. Not a lie at all.

Emma nodded, her eyes wide and eager. "Sounds exciting."

"Not as exciting as meeting you."

Emma smiled and shied away, looking down at her lap and running her fingers over her evening bag. The crowd had filled the room, the conversation at a steady din, broken only by the introduction of a thumping beat of dance music. The lights went down and the volume grew louder, the bass reverberating in Daniel's hips and thighs. Or perhaps that was Emma's effect on him. He had an amazing vantage point sitting next to her, one where he could admire the dips and valleys of her collarbone and shoulders. She had exquisite skin. Touchable and shimmery. How badly would he jeopardize his family business if he asked an Eden's employee out for dinner?

The models began to strut down the catwalk, which would normally catch Daniel's attention, but Emma was the real attraction. She leaned into him. "Isn't it exciting?"

"It is." He found himself smiling, of all things. That was not his usual reaction when forced to attend an event like this.

"This is my first time coming to one of these."

Utterly charming—those were the words the came to mind. "I never would've known. You seem like an old pro."

She reached over and swatted his thigh with the back of her hand. Now the grin on his face felt as though it might never leave.

Emma studied the models and applauded, her enthusiasm for fashion seeming so genuine. Her face was full of wonder as she followed each new design down the runway. Watching her became Daniel's primary source of entertainment, especially as she pointed out her favorites.

"Ooh. I love that one," she whispered in his ear. The hint of warmth from her sweet breath brought every nerve ending alive, like flipping on a switch.

"It's lovely." *You're lovely.*

She repeated this exercise over and over again, muttering comments into his ear whenever she found a particular design detail interesting. As the show went on, she seemed to become even more comfortable with him, leaning in closer. The conversation continued, and he found it was easier to hear her if he slung his arm across the back of her chair. She placed her hand on his thigh, sending signals straight to his groin. He wanted her. He wanted to take her home. But he had work to do after the show was over. Important work he couldn't afford to miss.

When the designers and several models made their final procession, Emma was one of the first in the audience to shoot to her feet and applaud wildly. Daniel was even more entranced. He loved her lack of inhibition. He was intrigued by the possibilities of getting Emma into his bed.

"I take it you enjoyed yourself?" he asked as the music died down and the crowd began to filter out of the room. From the corner of his eye, he saw Nora Bradford walking away. He couldn't let her out of his sights, but he wasn't ready to excuse himself from Emma. He needed her number. He deserved a little fun while he was in New York. No strings attached, of course.

"It was amazing. The clothes were incredible. It's definitely been the most exciting part of my job to date."

Daniel wasn't sure how much he should dig into Emma's life at Eden's. He dreaded learning anything that might indicate she was not a woman to pursue. He wanted her, but he wouldn't risk everything to take her to bed.

"One more drink?" he asked, unwilling for this to be goodbye.

"Yes. Please." Emma answered instantly and smiled widely, momentarily numbing him to his sense of duty to his family business. Daniel knew where a second drink might lead, or at least where he wanted it to go, and that was not a good idea. He had unfinished business tonight. And it didn't involve the stunning woman from Eden's department store.

Emma worried for more than a moment that she'd answered too quickly. Daniel was all suave sophistication, and she'd been nothing but goofy with excitement during the fashion show. She wasn't sure what had come over her, except that she felt different right now. For the first time, she felt as though she could be comfortable in this world. More importantly, she could hold her own with a handsome man like Daniel.

"Shall we?" Feeling a bit invincible, she hooked her arm in his and snugged him close to her.

The look he cast down at her shook her to her core. So confident. So pleased. So hot. "Please."

Emma took a step and her shoe caught on the carpet. It twisted right off her foot and she stumbled forward.

Daniel kept her from falling with a strong hold on her arm. "Are you okay?"

Embarrassment heated her cheeks, but she was determined to make a graceful save. A little hiccup was not going to ruin her evening. "I'm great. Just need to get my shoe." She reached down to hook her finger into a silver strap, but as she bent at the waist, she felt a pop behind her. Cool air hit the center of her back. She still needed her shoe, so she crouched to grab it. In a rush, the cold spread down her spine. *The zipper.*

She let go of Daniel's arm, righted herself and immediately flattened her back against his chest, clutching her dress to her bosom with one hand and her shoe in the other. The fine wool crepe of his tuxedo brushed against her bare skin. Her zipper had split wide-open. The only thing that was keeping the dress on was that impossibly tiny silver hook at the very top and the few inches of bodice before the skirt started.

"Everything all right?" Daniel grasped her shoulders from behind and looked down at her.

Emma's chest was heaving. Panic coursed through her veins. Of course something disastrous would happen. "My zipper. I think it broke." She knew one thing as soon as those words came out. The humiliation of this scene was going to last her entire lifetime. She'd have to start taking the stairs in her apartment building. She might have to move.

Daniel pushed her shoulders forward ever so slightly. "Indeed it has."

That small breach of the space between them told her exactly how bad it was. Daniel could see far more of her than was reasonable for the first few hours of their acquaintance. Her bare back. Her skimpy panties. "Do you think you can fix it?" Luckily, most people had made it back out into the reception area. The few still milling about didn't seem to notice. "I can't walk out of here with half a dress."

He pulled her a little closer and lowered his head. "No. But we could stay in here with half of your dress." His breath was warm against the slope of her neck.

She craned her head, looking at him over her shoulder. His lips were so close, achingly within reach. If they were somewhere quiet and private, this mishap could've been the perfect icebreaker. Her clothes were already half off. Might as well go all the way. "As fun as that sounds, I'm still going to need to walk through that room at some point."

"Hold on. Let me see if I can do anything." He

waited as a few people walked past, then he made more space between them.

Emma tried very hard to not think about how much he was essentially studying her naked back and every inch of lacy undergarments that went with it. "Well? How bad is it?"

"From where I'm standing, the view is spectacular." He traced his finger along one edge of the zipper, his warm skin brushing hers. It had been so long since a man had touched her like that, and certainly no man as sexy and handsome as Daniel.

"You get bonus points for flattery." *And for making me dizzy.* "I'd still like to know if the dress can be saved."

"The two sides of the zipper aren't attached anymore. It's just the hook holding it together."

Emma didn't know a lot about garment construction, but she did know that there was no saving that stupid zipper. "What do I do? I didn't bring a jacket or coat."

"I did." Daniel stepped back and shrugged his shoulders out of his tuxedo jacket. Emma got a much better sense of his body now that it was hiding under fewer clothes. If she wasn't so deathly embarrassed, she might be daring enough to invite him home. He placed his jacket on her shoulders and held her shoe and handbag as she slipped her arms inside.

"This is so nice of you."

"Think nothing of it."

Emma sat in a chair and worked her foot into her shoe. "I'm not accustomed to such chivalry." Not even close. Her only real boyfriend had been the sort of guy who didn't want to share his umbrella in the rain.

"Still care for a drink?"

Emma stood, well aware that whatever magic she'd managed to conjure this evening would evaporate if she was the woman walking around in a broken dress and tuxedo jacket. "It's probably best if I head home." She could hardly believe the words. He was too amazing. She was missing her chance. Hopefully, she'd have another, perhaps run into him in the building again.

He nodded. "I understand. There's someone I need to track down, anyway. Let me walk you to your car, though."

Emma pulled out her phone and sent a text to Mindy's driver, who said he could be out front in a few minutes. The disappointing end of this evening was unimaginable, but she was determined to steal a few more lovely moments with Daniel. "That would be nice."

"Don't worry. I won't let anything bad happen." He placed his arm around her shoulder and walked her through the double doors.

They wound their way through the crowd. Several people gave her funny looks, but she did her best to hold her head high. Daniel's presence certainly made it easier. He ushered her outside, where the red carpet photographers were lying in wait. As soon as she was spotted, the flashes started going off. Yet another thing she had not bargained on.

Emma squinted as the bright lights made it hard to

see. A black SUV pulled up to the curb and Mindy's driver rounded the back of the car, waiting for her on the sidewalk.

"That's my ride," she said.

Like the perfect gentleman, Daniel escorted her to the waiting car, and Emma climbed into the back seat. As soon as she was inside, she started to remove his jacket.

He held up his hand. "Please. Keep it."

"No. It's okay. I know you have to go back in and find someone." She had to wonder who he was meeting. Surely there were hundreds of women in that room who would love even a moment with Daniel. Still, Emma was immensely grateful for the time she'd had with him, even with the way it was ending.

He slid his hand onto her shoulder and gave a subtle squeeze. Even through the suit fabric, it was wonderful. "I'm the only person who has seen the state of your dress. When you arrive home, I'd like you to be able to retain your dignity."

She smiled. "That's so sweet."

"Oh, I have my reasons. If you keep it, it'll give me an excuse to see you again."

Emma's face flushed so quickly she was surprised she could still sit up straight. "You're forcing me to hold your jacket hostage?"

He leaned in even closer. Good God, she wanted him to kiss her. She found herself puckering just to extend the invitation. "Part and parcel of being a gentleman."

The car behind hers honked. She jumped. Daniel grimaced and looked back.

"I should go," she said, hoping he'd protest.

"I'll need your number if I'm going to see you again."

His voice was a bit desperate and that was when the realization hit her—he didn't recognize her from their building. Looking back at the first thing she'd said to him tonight, she was shocked by her own brazenness. That had been a far bolder gesture than the real Emma would have ever made.

"So you *really* don't know who I am? I don't look the slightest bit familiar to you?"

"I'm so sorry. Should I know who you are?"

She laughed quietly, but it was more born of sad resignation than happiness. He hadn't noticed the everyday Emma. Not at all. She leaned over and placed a kiss on his cheek. She desperately hoped that wouldn't be the extent of things between them, but if it was, at least the end could be on her terms. She'd either be bold Emma and go to his apartment, or she'd be her old self and leave the jacket with the doorman and attempt to hide from Daniel forever. First, she needed time for her ego to feel a little less bruised.

She reached for the door handle. "Don't worry, Daniel. I'll find you."

And just like that, the driver pulled away from the curb and sped off into yet another magical big city night. Emma wrapped her arms around herself and sat back in the seat, looking off through the window, wondering what was ahead for her and her slightly-less-mysterious Mr. Brit. Romance? At least a real kiss? Or was tonight as good as it would ever get?

Four

Mindy Eden knew she had to make a change. She nudged Sam Blackwell, trying to wrench him from his peaceful post-sex slumber. Yes, they'd had a white-hot night after they'd skipped the Empire State fashion show, but Sam took chances Mindy wasn't always comfortable with. In the elevator on the way up to her apartment last night, he'd slipped his hand under her skirt while a couple from her building rode along with them. He'd blocked any view with his jacket strategically draped over his arm, and she'd nearly had an orgasm while he pleasured her. It was fantastic, but it was not right. Mindy didn't like herself when she was like this, making rash decisions and not caring about consequences.

But Sam did that to her. He made her do stupid,

stupid things. All the more reason to make a pre-emptive strike. "Sam. I think you should go." She shook his shoulder again. He rolled away from her, his breaths quickly becoming soft and even.

Simply saying that she wanted him to go made her remorseful. She didn't really want him to leave. She wanted him to stay, for real, just spend a day with her. But she'd learned by now that expectations like that were foolish with Sam. He was always on to the next thing, hopping on his private plane and jetting off to another corner of the world. There was always more money to be made, another deal to strike. She worried there might even be other women. How could there not be? With his square jaw, dark eyes and thick tousled hair, he could have any woman he wanted. Never mind the billions he had in the bank. For most women, Sam would be impossible to resist, even if he were penniless. She had no proof he was romancing anyone else. It was more a hunch, a little voice at the back of her head asking one simple question—*Why do you trust this guy?*

Her sister Sophie certainly didn't trust him. Neither did Sophie's fiancé, Jake. Sam had a reputation for being an unscrupulous businessman. He would do anything to succeed. He had a knack for finding other people's weak spots and taking advantage. In Mindy's case, her weak spot was her neck. One brush of Sam's lips and she was putty in his hands. It took very little effort for him to get her into bed. She'd learned that hours after meeting him, five months ago.

Knowing he'd wake up at the prospect of more sex,

she slid closer to him, pressing her breasts against his broad back, cupping his firm shoulder with her hand and rubbing his calf with her foot. "Sam. Please wake up," she whispered against his neck. She tried very hard not to inhale his smell, but she couldn't resist. She liked it too much.

He rolled to his back, a cocky smile crossing his lips while his eyes remained shut. "I don't usually perform sex on demand, but in your case, I'll make an exception."

"That's not what I was asking." Her nipples grew hard at the mere suggestion, heat pooling between her legs. She wanted him. Again.

He reached around and grabbed her bottom, giving it a gentle squeeze. "Then maybe *I* should ask. I want you, Min. One more time?"

Mindy knew she had to be strong. "I don't think that's a good idea. I don't think we're a good idea anymore, Sam."

He opened his eyes, a flash of dark sexiness that was a verifiable shot to the heart. "What's wrong? Didn't we have fun last night?"

Mindy sat up in bed and pulled the rumpled sheets against her chest. "We did have fun. But that's all we ever have and I should be focusing on work. I blew off an important industry event because of you last night. You're a distraction."

He propped himself up, his elbow on the pillow. "You need a distraction. You work hard and are in an impossible situation." Under the covers, he caressed her inner thigh, starting at her knee and moving north, the tips of his fingers dangerously close to her center. He knew exactly how to manipulate her.

Still, she ached for more of his touch. She ached for all of him—body and soul. That was the problem. All he offered was the former, never the latter. "I know how hard I work. I eat stress for breakfast, lunch and dinner." It was the truth. Before she'd inherited one-third of Eden's, she already had a wildly successful company of her own, By Min-vitation Only, an on-line greeting card and invitation design and printing service. Although she'd hired an interim CEO for BMO, she was still involved in the day-to-day, all while performing her duties at Eden's. She could be stretched only so far.

"I offered to get rid of the obligation you don't want."

She shook her head. "And I told you no. Don't you dare sabotage Eden's. Sophie and Emma would never forgive me."

"Why? You'd all lose some money, but you'd also all be out from under the burden of that business. Plus, it's a drop in the bucket compared to what you'd be left with. The real value of Eden's is the building and the land it sits on."

This was an argument Mindy had wholly embraced six months ago, when Gram died unexpectedly and Mindy knew she and Sophie were set to inherit the business. But the terms of the will were such that the heirs, Mindy, Sophie and Emma, had to run the business together in good faith, for two years. Mindy might be driven to protect her own best interests, but she couldn't turn her back on her sisters. She couldn't thumb her nose at her grandmother's wishes.

"We've been through this one hundred times." She climbed out from under the covers and grabbed her silk robe from a hook on the closet door. "Logic says you're right, but I have to be a good person. That means working like a dog for two years and hopefully being able to sell my interests in Eden's to my sisters when that time is up. I might be stuck, but it's not forever."

"Why be stuck at all?"

"Because I'm loyal to my family."

Sam shrugged and threw back the covers. The sight of his naked muscled form made her breath catch in her chest. "You worry too much about what other people will think."

Again, Sam had a talent for zeroing in on Mindy's weaknesses. She did worry about what Sophie thought. She wasn't so sure what to make of Emma. She wasn't sure she could trust her to do a good job at Eden's. Mindy and Sophie had known her for only a few months in the context of sisterhood and partnership. Emma had largely been a disappointment. She didn't have a nose for big business strategy. She certainly didn't have a nose for fashion.

Mindy's phone rang with the ring tone she'd assigned to Sophie. "I have to get this. If my sister is calling at seven in the morning, something's wrong." She lunged for her cell as it buzzed on the nightstand. "Soph, hey. Two seconds, okay?" She pressed the button to mute the call.

"I'm going to hop in the shower. Join me when you're done?" Sam casually placed his hand against the jamb of the bathroom doorway, flaunting his unbelievable body. She didn't need to touch him. She could see how hard he was.

"Give me a minute and I'll be there."

"Don't be long. I need you, Min."

I need you, too, Sam. Precisely the reason she had to make a change.

Daniel didn't wait for his alarm clock the morning after Empire State. He'd hardly slept at all. Visions of sexy, enchanting Emma tormented him. She was a feast for the senses, beautiful, sweet smelling and impossibly soft to the touch. If he could afford to put any time at all into seduction, he might pursue her with everything he had. But there was no room for distractions while he was in New York, and especially not of the female variety. Daniel had a real talent for finding women who at best made his life impossibly complicated, and at worst, broke his heart. His family was counting on him. He had to prove that he could fill the void left behind by William.

Still, it was tough getting Emma out of his head. She'd surprised him at every turn last night. From the moment she so boldly introduced herself, she'd been nothing but refreshingly candid and at ease. She did not put on airs or try to impress him. She hadn't boasted once of her family lineage or about important people she knew. He still wasn't sure what to make of her, especially after her parting comment: *Don't worry, Daniel. I'll find you.* How, exactly, would she do that?

The sun was beginning to peek between the drapes and the dogs were beginning to stir. There was no point in pretending he'd get any sleep at all, so he tossed back the covers and dressed for his morning walk with the dogs. With all three on their leashes, he took the elevator down to the lobby and made his way across the street to Central Park. They completed their usual circuit, then Daniel made his last stop at a newsstand a block away. Call him old-fashioned, but he didn't enjoy reading the news on a computer screen or tablet. He preferred the feel of real paper. He didn't think twice when reaching for *The Times*, but the large print of a tabloid made him stop short.

Retail Royalty Romance!

There, beneath the juicy headline, was a picture of himself and Emma as she placed a kiss on his cheek. Shock and heat coursed through him in equal measure as he was confronted with the visual evidence of one of last night's most memorable moments. He read the headline again. The British press had long referred to the Stone family as retail royalty. He was outed now. His mother was going to lose it.

He wasn't about to read more out on the street, so he paid for his purchases and rushed back to his building, dogs in tow. Daniel rushed into the waiting elevator and jabbed the button for his floor, willing it to travel faster. He peered at the picture on the front page again. He was *leaning* into the kiss, his hand at Emma's waist. Despite the fact that it hadn't been on the lips, the photograph was nothing less than sexy. Of course it was—she was too stunning for words.

Inside his apartment, he tossed his keys aside and let all three dogs off their leashes. They bolted into the kitchen for water. Daniel took his papers and plunked down on the sleek black leather sofa in the living room. He flipped to the full story inside. It took only a few words for him to learn why Emma had been so flabbergasted that he hadn't known who she was.

She was one of the Eden heiresses. A beautiful billionaire. He wasn't the only member of a royal retail family. They both were. *Bloody hell.*

He studied the other photographs. One was of her on the red carpet, spinning her skirt up in the air like a model, revealing her lithe legs. There was a second one of himself with Emma during the show, apparently snapped by someone with a camera phone. His arm was slung across the back of her chair. Her legs were crossed, that unforgettable dress cut dangerously high up her silky thigh. He saw how focused he was on her as she whispered in his ear. If this was any other woman on the planet, he might not feel so stupid about how distracted he'd been by her. But Emma was trouble. She was an Eden.

How had he managed to not only meet the one woman he had no business spending time with, but also let her run off with his tux jacket? He hadn't simply waded into treacherous waters with an Eden heiress, he'd found a stretch of shark-infested sea.

His phone buzzed in his pocket. It was certainly

his mother. She'd stopped reading the papers after his brother's accident, especially when the press figured out that William, and Daniel's former fiancée, Bea, had been having an affair. Their mother had been too embarrassed, and unwilling to believe it. But she had plenty of people at the Stone's office in London feeding her information. It was now time for damage control. "Hello, Mum."

"It looks as though you had a good time at Empire State."

"You've seen the papers."

"Was this a calculated move on your part?"

"It wasn't, but seems like an awfully good stroke of luck."

The other end of the line became eerily quiet, so much so that Daniel wondered if the connection had been dropped. "I fail to see how this could possibly be good," she finally said. "The Eden family is poison."

"I'm not sure of that. Emma is lovely. And she undoubtedly knows quite a lot about her family's business." All of that was the truth, but he was well aware he was covering his own ass.

"So you're after information?"

He hadn't known until moments ago that it was an option, but it wasn't a bad idea, especially if it meant spending time with Emma. "Seems like I ought to try, doesn't it?"

"Do you think she'd actually trust you? How do you know she won't lie to you?"

"I don't. But I'd like to think I'm a good judge of character."

"One could argue that you're a bit blind when it comes to women, Daniel."

He bristled at the suggestion. He hadn't been blind to the fact that William and Bea had fallen in love behind his back. He'd only been stupid enough to hope his own brother would do the right thing and back off. "This is just business. Information is power. You know that as well as anyone."

"And you've handed it to the enemy on a silver platter. You've blown your cover. Everyone knows you're in New York scouting locations for Stone's. There's no telling what the Eden sisters will do to try to stop us."

Daniel's shoulders tightened with every damning detail she launched at him. He knew his predicament. He didn't need her constant reframing of the problems. "We should have been up front about it from the beginning. If you're going to compete, better to do it out in the open where everyone can see."

"This isn't a competition, Daniel. It's war."

He shook his head. How his mother loved to cling to her Eden's grudge. "It doesn't matter what you call it. Stone's will succeed. I promise you that."

"I'm not sure you're in a position to make guarantees."

He wasn't, but he'd never admit defeat until he'd run out of options. Right now, he had many directions he could take this, and he intended to do exactly that. "Everything is proceeding according to plan."

She tutted on the other end of the line. "Alright

then. But stay out of the papers. At least until we've signed a lease."

"I'll do my best, but you know how the press is."

"Yes, dear. I do."

Daniel hung up the phone, relieved his mother had forgotten about the most pressing task from last night—speaking to Nora Bradford. Daniel had been unable to track her down after seeing Emma off in her car. He couldn't afford to call her office and leave a message. Someone would figure out what he was up to. He was going to have to find a different way.

He began pacing in his living room. He needed to formulate his next several moves. If anyone asked, he was going to have to hedge his answers about Stone's opening their first US store in New York. As for Emma, pursuing her even for a fling would do nothing but create problems. But as he thought about her naked back, the channel of her spine and those lacy panties she'd been wearing last night, he couldn't deny that he wanted her. Perhaps there was some truth in the value of keeping your friends close. And your enemies closer.

Emma stared off at the city as she rode in the back of her black Escalade on the way to work. Her inability to focus was surely from no sleep after Empire State last night, and that was all because of Daniel. He was everything she'd never been able to find in a man—easy on the eyes and a true gentleman. It was hardly fair that his rich British accent came in a package six feet and several more inches tall. His manner and pure refinement made him seem too good to be true. But *someone* had saved her from a lifetime of embarrassment last night, and she had the tux jacket back at her apartment to prove it.

When she arrived home last night, she'd considered grilling Henry, her building's doorman, for Daniel's apartment number. She'd considered showing up on his doorstep, returning his jacket and asking him to undo the tiny hook that was holding up her dress. She'd fantasized about loosening Daniel's tie, unbuttoning his crisp, white shirt and spreading her hands across his broad chest...

But she had done none of those things.

He had gone to meet someone, presumably another woman. Never mind that Emma wasn't a woman who took charge, especially not when it came to unbuttoning. Her history with men was limited and disappointing—she'd gone to bed with only one, and he'd been such a jerk about her inexperience, telling her that a woman should know what to do without needing to ask him. Emma wasn't a mind reader. She'd only wanted someone who could be patient with her.

Plus, she was foolishly glossing over the most upsetting revelation from last night. Daniel hadn't recognized her from the elevator in their building. He'd taken notice only once she was wrapped up in a ten-thousand-dollar gown, and made up by two professionals who'd devoted an hour to the pursuit. But everyday Emma, with her freckles and propensity to babble when she got nervous? He hadn't noticed her at all. That told her all she needed to know. Daniel the mysterious Brit would never let her take off his shirt. She was out of his league.

The Escalade rounded the corner onto Thirty-Seventh Street and pulled up in front of Eden's. A cluster of people with cameras were waiting by the central revolving doors.

"What the heck?" she muttered to her driver, Gregory. "I wonder if they got a tip about a celebrity shopping at the store this morning."

"I don't like the looks of this. Do you want me to drive around to the south entrance, Ms. Eden?" Gregory asked.

Emma waved it off. "No. It's fine. They're not interested in me."

Gregory exited the car and rounded to her door as she hopped out onto the sidewalk. The photographers swarmed her. All she could see were cameras and arms and faces.

Emma! Emma!

Are you and Daniel Stone dating?

Did you know he's opening a store in New York?

They barked their questions, shouting her name. Gregory begged them to stand back so she could get into the building unscathed. She shuffled across the sidewalk in heels, while everything they'd just said hit her. Dating? Mr. Brit? It had to be. How many Daniels had she been seen with? Exactly one.

Gregory blocked the photographers from getting into the store while Emma ducked through the revolving door. Duane, the hulking head of Eden's security, was lumbering toward her, hitching up his belt and looking frazzled. "Ms. Stewart. I'm so sorry. I chased two photographers away from the south entrance, but I had to stay and deal with the shoppers lined up to get into the store."

"Shoppers?" Emma kept walking toward the executive elevator bank, Duane at her side. "Do we have an event this morning?"

"So you don't know?"

"Know what?" Was she really so out of the loop that the head of security knew more about the goings-on in the store than she did?

"You're the event, Ms. Stewart." Duane jabbed the button to call the elevator. "You. Your dress. Your date last night. Those women outside are lined up to buy the dress you wore to Empire State."

With a ding, the doors slid open, but Emma was frozen in place. "I'm sorry. What did you say?"

Duane held the elevator and ushered her on board. "It sounds like you need to see the papers. I need to get back to the crowd outside. Only five minutes until the store opens."

"Papers?" Emma muttered to herself as she made the short ride upstairs. The instant she stepped off the elevator, Lizzie popped up from her seat. "Mindy and Sophie are waiting for you."

At this point, this came as no real surprise. Thank goodness Duane had given her a heads-up. "Is this about the photographers downstairs?"

Lizzie nodded. "And the tabloids."

It was all starting to come together. Sheer horror shuddered through her. Had someone managed to get a photo of her dress split wide-open? That was *not* the fashion statement her sisters had hoped for her to make. For the second day in a row, she marched into Sophie's office.

"Feeling better?" she asked Sophie. Emma was legitimately concerned, but she was also stalling. She didn't want bad news to end the spell of last night.

"Something I ate. I'm sorry I left you in the lurch with Empire State."

Mindy, who was sitting in a chair opposite Sophie's desk, crossed her legs and tutted. "I am not the lurch."

Uh. Yes you are. Emma wanted to say it so badly as she took the other chair. "You did leave me alone in a room full of hundreds of people."

Mindy slid a newspaper from Sophie's desk and casually tossed it into Emma's lap. "You didn't seem to have any problem making friends."

Emma could feel the deep crinkles forming on her forehead. There before her was a photograph of her kissing Daniel on the cheek. She could see her own fingers curling into his biceps. How one photograph could convey so much longing, she wasn't sure. Hopefully, it was only her interpretation and not the way the rest of the world saw it. "Wait a minute. How long have you two known about this? Why did nobody call me?"

"We were strategizing," Sophie said. "Trying to figure out what Daniel Stone is up to."

"Up to? What does that mean? You know him?" Emma tried very hard to squash down her hurt feelings. Mindy and Sophie were a unified front and Emma was the third wheel.

Mindy turned to her and shook her head. "You really don't know who he is, do you? Or *what* he is, to be more exact? He's a Stone."

Confusion whirled in Emma's head. "I'm sorry. A stone?"

Sophie bugged her eyes as if she couldn't believe Emma was so dense. "Stone's of London. Department store? The biggest in Europe? They're the reason Eden's was never able to get off the ground overseas."

"I've never even heard of it. This guy is part of the company?" Her vision returned to the paper and she opened it up to the main article. As she read, the weight of this hit her. "Oh. Wow. They think he's opening a department store in New York?"

"Why else would he be here?" Sophie asked. "Jake did some digging and found out that Daniel's been looking at commercial real estate properties. His agent is Charlotte Locke. She's the sister of one of Jake's closest business associates."

"He's been looking at big properties," Mindy added. "Definitely big enough for a department store."

"What does this mean? Could they put us out of business?" It would be just Emma's luck that she would essentially win the life lottery by meeting a guy as sexy as Daniel, only to have everything crumble to dust in her hands.

"They could not only put us out of business, that's likely their sole aim. Daniel's mother hated Gram. My guess is he cozied up to you last night for information," Sophie said.

"But I approached him."

"You did?" Mindy asked, incredulous.

"He lives in my building. I recognized him from the elevator. Don't forget that I was all alone in a room full of five hundred strangers." Emma sank back in her seat. "There's no way he talked to me because I'm associated with Eden's. He didn't even know who I was." She picked at a spot on her pants. "I don't even think he recognized me at all. That's how memorable I am. Apparently."

"He's playing dumb," Sophie asserted. "He's up to something. I know it."

Lizzie poked her head into Sophie's office. "Sorry to interrupt, but there's been a run on the designer department downstairs. We've completely sold out of the dress Emma wore last night."

"Hey. That's something." Emma sat a little straighter, proud of herself for doing something positive for the store.

"Also, Emma," Lizzie continued. "Daniel Stone is on the line for you."

Emma's heart was now residing in her throat. Apparently today was capable of getting exponentially more bizarre.

"Like I said. Up to something." Sophie seemed entirely convinced of her theory.

Emma still wasn't buying it. If he did know who she was, he'd done a convincing job of being nothing but a gentleman who didn't remember her. "What do I do?"

"Take the call," Mindy said. "We'll put him on speaker in here."

Emma shook her head. She'd had enough of Mindy and Sophie treating her as if she had no autonomy. "I'll take it in my office." She got up from her chair and met Lizzie at the door.

"You can't keep this from us," Sophie pleaded. "If you talk to him, we need to know what you're talking about."

"You two sent me into that fashion show on my own and I'm the reason there are women buying up Nora Bradford dresses downstairs. I've earned the right to speak to Daniel on my own. Trust me, I'm not going to let him do anything bad to Eden's." She turned to Lizzie. "Please put him through."

"Right away."

Emma hurried into her office, her mind and body buzzing with anticipation and excitement and more than a little worry. What if Daniel really was cozying up to her to get information about Eden's? What if he was out to destroy them? She didn't have time to think about the what-ifs. She had to answer the phone. "Good morning." She feigned as much confidence as she could.

"Good morning, Ms. Stewart."

Emma sat back in her chair, relishing the way the sound of his voice made her feel lighter and warmer. She could get used to hearing him say those four words, especially if he whispered them across the pillow. "Calling about your jacket? I told you I'd get it to you."

"I'm phoning because I embarrassed myself last night. Now I know what you meant when you asked if I knew who you were. I'm sorry I didn't realize you were one of the Eden heiresses."

Emma laughed quietly. "That's not how you should have known me. I'm by far the lesser known of the three. Most people have no clue who I am, Mr. Stone."

"Please call me Daniel."

"Only if you call me Emma. And like I said, most people don't know who I am."

"I'd say that's their loss." His voice was low and even a bit gravelly. Emma's mind flew to the photograph of their kiss on the cheek. She should have gone for it and planted one on his very sexy mouth, especially if those were the kinds of words that were going to come out of it.

"It's okay. I prefer to hang back."

"That's not what your dress suggested."

"It's not my habit to let my zipper split open at a fashion show."

Now it was his turn to laugh. She realized how much she loved the sound, which was not a good development. Mindy and Sophie might be right. What if Daniel Stone was up to no good? "I just happened to be the lucky bloke who witnessed it."

Heat bloomed across her face. It felt as if her cheeks were on fire. "That was a one-time occurrence, hopefully. Just like I'm hoping that you hiding your true identity from me won't happen again."

He cleared his throat. "You didn't tell me your whole story, either."

"I told you I work for Eden's. That much is true." She still felt that way, like she was an employee and not a real part of the team. Not even her newfound wealth made her feel like an Eden. While Mindy and Sophie continued to tell her what to do and micromanage her, she would always feel like that.

"You own a third of the Eden empire. You're far more than an employee. I could ask what your motives are. After all, you approached me."

Motives. That was the most pressing question between them, wasn't it? Was Daniel Stone up to something nefarious? The mere thought of answering his question made Emma's heart thump harder. "You want the truth?" She could hardly believe she'd offered.

"Always." His British accent and smooth delivery were chipping away at her resolve.

"I approached you because I was all by myself and you were by far the most handsome man in the room."

"I see."

"Does it disappoint you that it wasn't because you're a Stone?"

"Not at all. I always enjoy knowing where I stand." He was playing things quite close to the vest, which not only made Emma nervous, it made her curious.

"Don't we all?"

"I suppose that's true."

The gears in Emma's head were turning. She had to find out where she stood with Daniel. She had to find out what he was up to. If she played her cards right, Daniel Stone might end up being a real boon. It could give her the chance to learn more about an important competitor's plans. It would help her prove her worth to Mindy and Sophie, all while spending time with the sexiest man she'd ever met.

"I do feel as though I owe you the favor of returning your jacket in person. After all, you did rescue me last night." She smiled, lazily drawing her fingertips back and forth across her collarbone. If Daniel were to show up at her office right now, she'd have a hard time containing herself.

"It's what a gentleman would do."

"Is that what you are, Daniel? A gentleman?"

"I'm whatever you need me to be."

Emma doubted that greatly. "When can I bring you your jacket?"

"I could come by your office? Maybe take you to lunch?"

Emma could think of nothing better, but she also didn't want Mindy and Sophie breathing down her neck. They were deeply suspicious of Daniel and his motives. Emma was concerned, of course, but she'd have been lying if she said that wasn't partially eclipsed by a deeper desire to see where their flirtation might lead. Mindy and Sophie both had exciting men in their lives, so why couldn't Emma? "I have a very full day today. Why don't I bring it by your place this evening? Does seven work?"

"Even better. If you give me your cell number, I can text you the address."

If Daniel was embarrassed by the fact that he hadn't known she was one of the three Eden heiresses, what she was about to say next was going to be a bit more painful. "I already know your address, Daniel Stone."

"Been doing a bit of your own detective work?"

"It wasn't hard. I live two floors below you."

Five

London traffic was considered some of the worst in the world, but Daniel was starting to think New York might have it beat. He pulled back the sleeve of his suit jacket to consult his Rolex. Six fifty-five. He was going to be late.

If Emma was a prompt person, and something told him she was, she would be waiting on his doorstep by the time he arrived. Between his tardiness and other missteps, he'd be surprised if Emma would wait for very long. Perhaps he'd arrive home only to find his jacket hanging on the doorknob of his apartment. One could argue that he hadn't been a *complete* ass. He'd rescued a woman in distress with his coat. He'd walked her to her car. He also hadn't realized she lived in the same building. If ever there was a sign that he was preoccupied with work, that was it.

"Sorry we're so jammed up in traffic, Mr. Stone." His driver made eye contact via the rearview mirror.

"Not your fault."

"At least it's not raining, right?"

Indeed, it had rained for much of the afternoon, but the night was clear and beautiful. At least his walk with the dogs later this evening would be a good one. "So right."

Another fifteen minutes and his driver pulled into the parking garage of his building. Daniel quickly bade him farewell and rushed to the bank of elevators, only to be stopped by Henry, the doorman.

"Mr. Stone. There's a problem. I tried to call you, but we must not have your correct cell number down here at the desk."

"Problem?" Daniel had already pressed the button for the elevator.

"Your dog walker never showed."

"What?"

Henry shrugged. "I'm just glad you got here. Hopefully, your apartment won't be too much of a mess."

Daniel blew out an exasperated breath. "Thank you, Henry. I appreciate the information. Remind me tomorrow morning to get you my mobile number."

"Will do."

The elevator dinged to announce its arrival and Daniel stepped on board, worrying twice as hard about what might be waiting for him upstairs. An angry Emma and an epic dog disaster? He arrived on his floor and the doors slid open. Emma was sitting on the leather-upholstered bench next to the elevator, his jacket draped over the seat next to her.

"I'm late. I'm so sorry," he said.

She rose to her feet, her eyes warm as they quickly found his. He felt stuck for a moment, grappling with the realization that he'd run into this woman in the building and hadn't noticed her. He was losing his touch.

"It's no problem. I tried to wait by your door, but the dogs kept barking." She gathered the jacket and looped it over her arm. "I didn't have a chance to have it cleaned. I hope that's okay. It's a beautiful jacket. I see that it has a Stone's label."

"Indeed. We carry only our store brand for menswear. It has quite a cult following." Daniel reached for the jacket, admonishing himself. He had no business sharing this information. He really had no business hoping the garment might smell like her. "This is perfect. Thank you."

Emma turned back to the elevator. "Okay, then. I guess I'll see you around the building? Maybe next time you'll remember me."

The dogs began to bark. They must have gotten a whiff of him. Pulled between his urgent obligation to them and wanting to at least make slight amends with Emma, he grabbed her arm. "No. Please. Don't go." He turned toward his own apartment. "Come with me? The dogs will quiet down once I'm inside. I'd like to talk."

A clever smile crossed her plump, raspberry-pink

lips. All he could think about was convincing her to break every zipper she owned. "Sure. I love dogs."

"Brilliant." Daniel opened his door, doing his best to calm his canine trio and keep them from jumping on his guest. "Slow down. It's okay. Daddy's home."

"That's so cute. Daddy." Emma snickered and closed the door.

Daniel had never once gone for cute. "I'm so sorry, but apparently the dog walker didn't show up today. Is there any chance you'd accompany me to the park for a few minutes so we can talk?"

Emma crouched down and Jolly went straight to her. "I have a few minutes, then I need to go."

Of course she did. She likely had a date. A woman like Emma did not sit home alone. Daniel deposited his laptop bag on the table in the foyer and grabbed the leashes from the hook. "We'd better get going then, shouldn't we?"

The instant they were in the confines of the elevator, he remembered meeting Emma the first time. Perhaps it was a recollection of her perfume, but the memory of her, and his poor behavior, rushed into his mind. "I'm so sorry I didn't recognize you the other night. I do remember meeting you. I held the elevator door, right?"

She pressed her lips together. "That was me."

"I'm so sorry. If you'd been wearing an evening gown that day I might have recognized you last night."

"You didn't find it strange I said that thing about how we had to stop meeting like that?"

He laughed. "I thought you were being a cheeky American."

"Just my attempt at being clever."

He reached out and touched her arm. "It was clever. Honestly, it works in either situation, strangers or someone you know. Of course, a line like that is always better delivered by a beautiful woman." He had no idea what had come over him. Only the old Daniel said openly flirtatious things and threw caution to the wind. He had to keep himself under control. "I'm sorry if that was forward."

"You've seen my undies. I don't think there's such a thing as forward at this point."

Heat bloomed in Daniel's chest, spread down to his waist and kept going, wrapping around his hips and thighs. Why had he not kissed her last night? He'd been a fool for not taking his chance, especially at a time when he hadn't known she was a member of the family his mother was dead set on destroying.

It was simply a beautiful night. The sidewalks were damp from the rain earlier in the day. The clip-clop of the horses drawing carriages around the park managed to rise above all other noise. She and Daniel crossed at the corner and walked one of the sweeping asphalt trails that meander through Central Park. She should have been happy to be with him, but once again, her nerves had returned. It'd been easy to convince herself earlier that she was capable of flirting with Daniel and gathering information about his business, but confronted with him in person, she knew how silly that notion was. She wasn't capable of being ruthless or heartless about anything. She simply wanted to get to know him, but she knew that anything she asked could be misconstrued as prying.

"Lovely night," he said, breaking the silence between them.

"It is." She frantically searched her mind for something else to say. She wanted to ask if there were nights such as this in London, but she didn't want him to know that she'd never been. Perhaps it was best to talk about the dogs. "What are their names?"

Daniel stopped near a bench while the dogs explored and marked some nearby shrubs. "The two Corgis are Mandy and Buckingham, Buck for short. The miniature English bulldog is Jolly." The second her name crossed his lips, the dog waddled over to Emma.

She crouched down to pet her. "She's adorable."

"She used to belong to my brother."

"How could he give up such a sweet dog?" Emma scratched Jolly behind the ears.

"It wasn't his choice. He was killed in a car accident."

Emma couldn't believe she'd put her foot in her mouth so badly. She should've been smart enough to at least look into Daniel's history after their phone call. She should've researched the Stone family and figured out who she was dealing with. This new world of hers was more conniving than she found normal. Everyday people did not need due diligence before a walk in the park. "I'm so sorry for your loss. When did it happen?"

"Not quite two years." They resumed their walk, deeper into the park.

"Was he older or younger?"

"Older by two years. My only sibling. He was the golden boy, so it's been an adjustment. There's no living up to William or his memory."

Emma could hear the pain in his voice. It went deep. "I'm sure that's not true."

"You haven't met my mother." Daniel cleared his throat. "What about you? Two sisters, right? Sophie and Mindy?"

So he *had* done his research. What if Mindy was right? What if Daniel did have ulterior motives? What if last night had been a trap and she'd walked right into it? "Half sisters. We have the same father. It's a long story." She was fairly certain that if Daniel had snooped, he would know the sordid details that were out there to be found. Everything else, the hush money paid to her mother for years, was well hidden.

"So I understand you're CFO for Eden's. That's far more important than a number cruncher." Every new detail he revealed made her more nervous.

"True."

"And how is the store doing since your grandmother passed away? Victoria Eden's memory must cast a very long shadow."

They'd officially arrived in uncomfortable territory for Emma. She didn't want to talk about this. She couldn't risk giving away a single secret. "We're doing our best. What about Stone's? I didn't realize you were considering a foray into the American market."

He nodded, looking down at the ground. "It's early days. No telling what will happen."

His answer was all evasiveness and that put Emma even more on edge. Spending time with Daniel and getting closer to him could be playing with fire. Sophie and Mindy had warned her. Unfortunately, the part of Emma that had the nerve to wear that dress last night was still dying to get out. She was so tired of playing it safe. She wanted a little fire in her life. And if she was going to get burned, she might as well do it with a scrumptious man like Daniel. "How long are you here in New York?"

"Three months, I think. I don't love it, but I'm learning to like it."

With any other man, that would be a strike against him. Emma had little patience for men who didn't stick around. Her father had certainly done that to her mom. But perhaps this was her safety net. She could have a fling and it wouldn't matter what happened. It would eventually end. Was the new Emma capable of getting close and not getting attached? The old Emma was not.

Too many conflicted thoughts were going through her head right now. She needed time and space to think. She liked Daniel a lot. But she wasn't sure it was a good idea to tempt herself. "I should probably head upstairs."

"I'll walk you. I don't like the idea of you walking the park alone at night."

Just when she'd been seeking distance in the name of her sanity, he offered more time together. More to the point, he was doing that chivalrous thing again. She had such a weakness for it. They turned back, but out of nowhere, Jolly bolted ahead. Her leash slipped from Daniel's hand. The bulldog scrambled off under the bushes.

Daniel took off after her, with the other dogs leading the way. "No! Jolly!"

Emma joined the pursuit.

Daniel arrived at a park bench and crouched down, peering behind it. "She loves to put me through my paces. I think she sometimes wants to remind me that I'm not her true master. Only my brother could fill that role."

Emma couldn't help but notice the bitter edge to Daniel's words, but there was a larger task at hand now, namely a small bulldog needing to be coaxed from out of the bushes. Emma got on all fours and made eye contact with Jolly. "Come here, sweetie. I won't hurt you." She snapped her fingers. Jolly took a small step, then shrank back.

"I'm worried she doesn't like living with me."

Emma snapped her fingers again and made a kissing noise. The dog took two steps this time, so Emma puckered up and made the noise again. Slowly, Jolly crept out from her hiding spot. Emma didn't move until the dog nudged her hand with her nose. "That's a good girl." She scooped up Jolly and tucked her under her arm. "Maybe I'll carry her inside."

Daniel stared at her in amazement. "How did you do that? The last time this happened, it was a half hour ordeal."

Emma relished her minor victory, even if once again Daniel had seen her in a less than ladylike position. "I worked for a dog groomer one summer." As soon as the words left her mouth, she worried that the answer made her seem too unrefined.

"Where did you come from, Emma?"

The question made her heart race. She wanted to tell him everything about her history, and how her father had left her and her mother dangling by a thread. Then again, she didn't. She refused to play the role of victim. After all, she had the entire world before her right now. Anything she could ever desire was at her fingertips. Maybe even Daniel. "Does it matter where I came from? I'm here right now."

He smiled and their gazes connected. Every bit of the electricity from last night was zipping back and forth between them again. "I…" He stepped closer. "I'm sorry. I'm sorry that I didn't remember you from the elevator."

"We hardly spoke."

"I remember it now. You made an effort. And I didn't. For that, I'm deeply sorry."

She touched his arm, the fabric of his suit jacket soft and smooth under her fingers. Her eyes were drawn to his face and not just because his eyes were so entrancing. There was so much more to admire, like his full lips and the way one side of his mouth wanted to twist higher than the other when he was amused. "I don't want you to feel bad, Daniel. Apology more than accepted."

He grinned and reached for her hand. Emma's pulse picked up, beating in double time. "You know, you aren't helping me at all. I thought it might be easier to ask you on a proper date if I was some way in debt to you."

A proper date? Emma had more than a few improper thoughts going through her head right now. "I'm the one who's in debt to you. If you hadn't given me your jacket, I might have left last night wrapped in a tablecloth."

"It could have been the biggest fashion statement of the entire event." Warmth radiated off him as they were again drawn closer. His fingers were wrapped snuggly around hers, his face close enough that she could see the darker flecks of blue in his incredible eyes.

"Maybe. Of course, I could ask *you* on a proper date. And then you wouldn't need to worry about needing a reason." So bold Emma really did exist. She just needed a bit of encouragement.

He scanned her face like he was searching for answers. Just as she'd already learned to expect, the right corner of his mouth went up. "And what about a reason for asking if I can kiss you? Do I need one of those?"

"A person can always ask." Emma bit down on her lip in eager anticipation. Was she going to get the kiss she should have had the sense to claim last night? "No guarantees on the answer. Although I'm definitely leaning toward yes."

His lips spread into a full smile, his breathtaking eyes crinkling slightly at the corners. "Yes?"

"I'll take it one further. Yes, please." Emma couldn't wait. Jolly tucked under her arm, Emma rose up onto her toes, leaning into Daniel. Her mouth met his and her body sprang to life. Her face tingled, her chest flushed with heat, her lips were nothing but hungry. When his lips parted and his tongue urged hers to do the same, she tilted her head even farther to the side, wanting everything she could get from him. The buzz of the city and the fresh smell of rain faded into invisible recesses as their kiss became the most powerful, living, breathing thing around them. His hand slid to the small of her back and Emma arched into him. She could already imagine how they would fit together in bed, and even though the idea intimidated her, just like she'd recently made so many other leaps, she wanted to jump ahead to that right now.

From under her arm, Jolly yipped. Emma was brought back to earth, reluctantly pulling her lips from Daniel's. "I don't think she likes us kissing."

His chest was rising and falling with each breath. She loved seeing that she'd gotten his pulse racing. She wasn't sure she'd ever had that effect on a man. "This would definitely be easier if I didn't have the dogs with me. I could take them back upstairs. Or you could come with me."

As tempting as his offer was, this was all moving

too fast. She wanted Daniel. But they'd known each other for a scant twenty-four hours, and their true identities for an even shorter amount of time. Plus there was the larger looming question of intentions. What were his? She wasn't sure she knew her own.

"I have a big day at work tomorrow. I should go." Everything Mindy and Sophie had said was ringing in her ears. Could she trust Daniel? Should she even be speaking to him? Her body and her mind warred while she struggled with the question. There was a chance she couldn't trust her sisters, either. They had their own agenda, and although it was undoubtedly intertwined with Emma's share of Eden's, they could throw her under the bus at any moment.

Daniel pressed his lips together and nodded. "I understand. I have quite a lot to accomplish tomorrow, as well. I'd still like to take you out if you're open to the idea."

Emma's heartbeat was beating so fast she wasn't sure how she was still standing. He wanted to see her again. "That would be lovely. What were you thinking?"

"I'm sure you've heard, but the English National Opera is performing *La Bohème* on Broadway over the next six weeks. It's opening Thursday night and I'm certain I can get us tickets. I've known the director for quite some time."

Emma pulse picked up again, sheerly out of nervousness. No, she hadn't heard. All these years living in close proximity to the city and she'd never seen a Broadway production, let alone the opera. Of course, she wasn't about to admit that. She couldn't imagine Daniel would be drawn to a woman whose world was as small as hers. Once again, she was going to have to fake it until she could make it. "That sounds lovely. I'd love to go."

A confident smile crossed his face and Emma had to wonder what it was like to walk around the world so self-assured. "Excellent. I'll secure the tickets."

What was the saying about playing with fire? That was how it felt to be with Daniel. He was unafraid to make an overture and kiss her in the middle of the park. He wasn't shy about asking her to the theater, all while there was a very good chance he intended to destroy her family's business. Despite his seeming sense of obligation to her, in the real world, Daniel owed her nothing. In some ways, that should scare her more than anything, but it also made the notion of Thursday night that much more thrilling.

"I can't wait."

Six

Daniel was not going to be late to pick up Emma for the opera. He gave himself plenty of time to jog down the two flights of stairs to her floor. Thinking about tonight, he was filled with the most puzzling mix of wariness and elation. Surely those two feelings were never meant to comingle in a sensible person's mind at one time, and he'd been feeling that way for two days. He'd tried to distract himself from thoughts of Emma by focusing on work, which was the perfect illustration of the push and pull in his life. He was drawn to Emma, but everything about her, her family and her career stood in direct opposition to his life.

Still, he was moving forward. Somehow. He'd found a space he quite liked for the New York location of Stone's this week. His real estate agent, Charlotte

Locke, was negotiating terms. If all went well, that would be sewn up soon. And he was moving forward with the date he'd asked Emma out on, even when he knew it wasn't a smart idea. Sometimes things don't make sense until later, he'd told himself. He had to listen to his gut, and it was telling him he'd miss out if he didn't at least test the waters with Emma.

He knocked and folded his hands before him, his heart beating fiercely in anticipation.

"Hey." Emma opened the door only a moment later, seeming flustered, almost panicked. "You're a little early." Her hair and makeup were perfect, but she was not dressed for a night out. She was wearing a short satin kimono-style robe, tied at the waist.

Daniel was mesmerized. "I'm sorry. Am I?" He fished his phone from his pocket and glanced at the home screen. Indeed, he was five minutes early.

Emma waved him in. "It's okay. I just need to finish getting dressed."

He trailed her into her apartment, enjoying the view of her bare legs and feet. "I'll just sit on the sofa and wait. Please don't rush on my account."

Emma turned to him and it was impossible not to notice the gentle swell of her breasts as her robe gaped slightly. He glimpsed just enough to make him wish he'd been unable to get tickets to tonight's performance. "Can I make you a drink?"

He held up his hand. He needed to stay on top of things this evening. "I'm fine, thank you."

"Okay. I just need a few minutes. Make yourself

at home." With that, Emma ambled down the hall and disappeared.

Daniel took the opportunity to explore her apartment. It was beautifully decorated in a neutral color scheme of snow white and creamy gray, with the occasional pop of pale pink and gold metal accents. Either Emma had a very refined sense of personal style or she'd paid a king's ransom to an interior designer. The apartment looked like a jewel box, straight out of a magazine.

He knew very little about Emma, and this trip through her abode wasn't providing many clues. There were no family photos, no real personal effects. He'd done a quick internet search since their visit to the park, but hadn't learned much, other than that Emma's place in the Eden lineage had been kept a secret for years. She'd been shipped off to France, apparently, to study in quiet, probably because of her father's affair. It was as if Victoria Eden had been hiding her granddaughter in an ivory tower. All the more reason not to trust Emma, however beguiling and gorgeous she was. But Daniel was certain he had everything in hand. He wouldn't let Emma get too close. He certainly wouldn't let her within the vicinity of his heart.

"I'm ready." Her voice was right behind him. Apparently she was light on her feet, like a cat.

Daniel turned and decided he couldn't care less about attending the opera. Emma was a vision in a sparkling black dress with skinny straps and a neckline that flaunted the same maddening view as her robe. Her skin shimmered as it had for Empire State, the light dancing off the enticing contours of her collarbone and cleavage. He didn't want to go anywhere. He wanted to stay here and kiss her again, let his lips roam everywhere. "You look beautiful. Like a princess."

"Thank you. Like retail royalty? If you believe what the tabloids say." She smiled and stepped closer, brushing the shoulder of his tux jacket. "You don't look too bad yourself."

"No need to worry about the tabloids this evening. I've made arrangements for us to duck into the theater through a back entrance without detection."

Disappointment crossed Emma's face. "Back entrance? That doesn't sound like much fun."

"It's the one a president or dignitary would use. I'm certain it's quite nice."

"I was hoping we'd end up in the papers again. Just like the other night, I'm wearing a Nora Bradford. She's one of Eden's exclusive designers. I'll earn big bonus points with my sisters if I can create another run on the store."

"Surely you realize it's not in my best interest to help Eden's." Nor was it in Daniel's best interest to help Eden's as pertained to Nora Bradford. He'd been unable to reach her, and his mother still didn't know about it.

"Of course not. But you can help *me*. The store and I are not synonymous."

She not only had an excellent point, Daniel felt the same way. His family was important, but he and the business were not the same thing. Still, his stomach churned at the prospect of going through the main entrance of the theater. He'd purposely avoided the red carpet at Empire State, although that had been for naught since he still ended up in the tabloids. "I'm sorry. I'm just not a fan of photographers or the media. They've treated me and my family badly in England." They'd been especially brutal once they figured out his brother and fiancée had been having an affair. It was too juicy for them to let it rest, so they'd kept the love triangle of his deceased brother, himself and the woman who'd betrayed him in the headlines for months.

"I don't want you to do anything you don't want to. I just..." Her voice trailed off.

"What is it?"

"My sisters. I'm trying to prove to them that I'm a real member of the team. That I can contribute."

Again, she was hitting all the right notes. It was exactly the way he felt about needing to prove himself to his parents. "You seem more than capable."

Emma shook her head, her eyes filled with a worry that tugged at his heart. "It doesn't matter. Mindy and Sophie are thick as thieves and they treat me like I'm an idiot sometimes. They see me as the outsider."

"But you're a blood relative."

She arched her eyebrows at him. "You've done your research."

"I have." He could admit that much. Didn't everyone do a Google search on anyone they might take on a date?

"Then you should know that Mindy and Sophie didn't know I was inheriting part of Eden's until the day our grandmother's will was read. I'm still earning their trust. They're still earning mine, for that matter."

"It really means that much to you? Going through the main entrance of the theater?"

"Unless you're worried that people will think we're dating. I wouldn't want to embarrass you." Her leading inflection did nothing but put him on the spot.

"The tabloids don't care about facts. They'll say whatever they want."

"As someone who's spent her entire life invisible to the public eye, I'm enjoying my moment in the spotlight. But if you'd prefer we hide, I'm okay with it."

Indeed, the Edens had hidden Emma away. It wasn't fair to her. She couldn't help that she'd been the product of an extramarital affair. He drew in a deep breath, realizing he wanted only to please her. He could stomach a few moments standing before the paparazzi and whatever headlines resulted from it. Just this once.

"We'll go in through the main entrance and see what happens."

"Really?" Emma's excitement was its own reward. Her cheeks colored in radiant pink. "Thank you so much."

"Of course." He'd forgotten how wonderful it was to make a woman happy. Would he have the chance to please Emma in other ways? He hoped so.

Daniel's driver was waiting for them downstairs in the parking garage.

"Why don't you ever have him pick you up out front?" Emma asked.

"Same reason I wanted to take the side door at the theater. It's a habit now. I do anything to retain my privacy."

"I see."

His driver had them to the theater quickly. It seemed like New York traffic was conspiring against him—whenever he had somewhere to be, it was nothing but gridlock. And when he was in no rush to confront what was awaiting him, like the chance of photographers, it was smooth sailing. They waited their turn in the line of limousines and town cars, but he could already see camera flashes going off. Opening night was always a big affair.

As soon as Daniel climbed out of the car, his pulse picked up and he waited for his stomach to sour. But then he reached for Emma's hand, her fingers slid against his palm, and a pleasant wave of warmth overtook him. He could do this. He had an extraordinary woman on his arm.

One photographer spotted them and the flashes started. Daniel and Emma weren't even on the red carpet yet and they were already a focus. Emma squeezed his hand. He wasn't sure if she sensed his trepidation or was expressing her own excitement. It didn't matter. He only knew that he wanted more. When they took center stage, the questions began.

Are you officially dating?

How did you meet?

Emma, what are you wearing?

Emma took a single step toward them and let go of Daniel's hand. "It's Nora Bradford, of course. We love her at Eden's." She turned to let them photograph the back of the dress while she peeked over her shoulder like a veteran of the red carpet. If he were inclined to enjoy this sort of thing, he'd be loving it right now. Watching Emma was the most fun he'd had in weeks. It was the photographers he disliked so greatly. "It's beautiful, isn't it?"

Daniel, is Stone's opening in New York?

How will the stores compete?

What do your families think?

Daniel had to admit that last question was an excellent one. He wasn't about to answer it. His mother had expressed more than enough concern. He was sure her sisters felt the same way. Emma snuggled herself tighter against his arm, smiling for the cameras and smartly ignoring the latest batch of questions. The photographers moved on to the couple behind them, a Hollywood actress and her husband, and Daniel tugged Emma into the theater.

"That wasn't so bad, was it? I think it's exciting." Indeed, she looked nothing short of exhilarated, her cheeks flushed with color and her eyes bright. "Thank you for putting up with that. I appreciate it."

"I'm just glad it's over." He didn't want to think about how what Emma had just done might end up dashing his hopes of signing Nora Bradford to Stone's. Forget damage control with his mother. She was going to hit the roof. For tonight, he wouldn't worry about it. He would instead enjoy his time with Emma.

They took their seats in the theater, the front row of one of the side boxes with an excellent view of the stage. Emma was perfectly at home here, among the women in evening gowns and men in tuxedos. However hidden away she'd been for much of her life, she'd surely been exposed to the finer things.

"These seats are amazing," Emma said. "I can't wait for the performance to start." Once again, he was taken aback by her enthusiasm. She enjoyed life, no matter how routine the moment. He could learn quite a lot from her.

The house lights went down. The orchestra began to play, exquisite music filling the theater. Emma turned her sights to the stage expectantly, practically sitting on the edge of her seat. When the curtains opened, she reached for Daniel's hand and squeezed hard.

He'd seen *La Bohème* many times, but never like this. Not with someone like Emma who so plainly appreciated it on a different level. Just like at Empire State, she openly displayed her enjoyment of the spectacle before her. Daniel had a difficult time keeping his eyes on the stage. It was much more beautiful and enchanting to watch it reflected in Emma's face, her eyes darting from side to side as she followed the performers, her luscious lips parted as she got caught up in the music.

And she wept, softly and sweetly, squeezing his hand tighter and letting the tears fall. Emma Stewart was a singular woman. She appreciated beauty in all its forms. She seemed to have nothing but the warmest of hearts and the most generous nature. If he wasn't careful, it wasn't a question of whether he would fall for her, but rather, how fast.

Daniel was intensely quiet on the ride back to their building. Emma was still composing herself after the performance. She hadn't wanted to embarrass him with her tears, but there was no holding any of it back, especially not at the end, when the music was so achingly beautiful and Rodolfo realized that Mimi had died. Though tragic, the story of poverty, sacrifice and love was wrapped up in such a spectacle, she couldn't have held back her emotion if she'd tried.

"I'm sorry about the tears. It was my first time seeing *La Bohème*. I guess I just got caught up in it." She didn't want to make an admission of her naivety, but she wanted to be honest with him. She didn't like always pretending to be something she wasn't.

He nodded, but she could see that look of surprise on his face. "That explains a lot. But there's no need to apologize. A lot of people cry."

Deep inside her was a desire to tell him more. She didn't like pretending to be something she wasn't, even when she knew her money and pedigree were part of what made him want to spend any time with her.

His driver dropped them in the parking garage. As they walked inside, she prepared herself for the awkward moment to come, when Daniel thanked her for accompanying him for the evening and then found a way to absolve himself of more time together. Perhaps this was the natural progression between a man like him and a woman like her. They were from different worlds. Warring families. But the fighter in her was unwilling to give up hope. She liked Daniel. She liked being with him—he had a way of making her feel like she was the only woman in the world. His focus was always on her. She'd never experienced that before. With anyone.

"Thank you for a lovely evening," she said, as the elevator opened.

Daniel waited for her to board first. She nearly choked on the quiet as the doors slid shut. He pressed the button for her floor—confirmation that there would be no invitation to join him upstairs. She was about to crumple in defeat when he turned to her with a gaze so intense it nearly knocked her over.

"It's you I have to thank, Emma. Tonight was extraordinary. I felt like I was seeing the performance for the first time, too. It's amazing to see the world through your eyes."

The elevator dinged and the doors opened. She had only seconds to act. She took his hand. "Don't go upstairs."

Daniel didn't take his eyes off her, but he thrust out his arm to keep the elevator open. "Are you sure?" His voice was soft and low. Intoxicating. "If I come over, I'll just want to kiss you again."

Her heart fluttered in her chest. "Good." Without a second to waste, she tugged him down the hall to her door. She felt like it was okay to breathe again until his eyes narrowed on her face. He set his hand on the side of her neck and ran a thumb across one cheek. That one innocent touch sent zaps of electricity through her. "You have freckles. How did I not notice that before?"

Her makeup had failed her. "I shouldn't have cried at the opera. It washed away my foundation. I must look horrible."

He shook his head. "You're stunning. It's okay to cry. It's beautiful. It's real. And moving."

Now her heart was thundering so much harder. He'd asked her the other night where she'd been hiding, but she was inclined to ask the same of him. He gathered her into his arms, pulling her close. She rose up onto her tiptoes. His kiss was soft and patient. A spark started a slow burn, his lips parting slightly, his tongue teasing when it touched hers. The anticipation might kill her. Not only had she never wanted a man the way she wanted Daniel, she hadn't known until that very moment what it was like to be desperate for someone and be in his arms at the same time. She was starving for more of him. All of him.

Emma fumbled with her keys, dropping them on the floor. Daniel bent over to pick them up, and she smoothed her hand across his broad shoulders, dying to know what his skin felt like, wanting nothing more than to touch him.

He opened the door and handed her the keys. She cast them aside on the foyer table, along with her clutch. Then she found his arms wrapping around her waist, and she clasped the sides of his face, his light facial scruff tickling her palms. He kissed her—

sensuous and slow, a pace that was pure Daniel. Emma was already on fire, consumed with desire. She wanted him out of his tailored tux. She wanted him to tear off her dress. She threaded her hands inside his jacket and urged it from his shoulders. He loosened his tie with one hand, but didn't let go of her with the other, his hot fingers curled into the bare skin of her back.

"I need to know if you want this, Emma."

Yes was waiting on her lips, but she was struck with a terrible case of nerves. Like everything else in her life, she was searching for a way to belong where she was, right now in the arms of the sexiest man she'd ever met. She absolutely wanted this. She wanted him more than anything, but she was scared of how he'd see her. She didn't want to be shy and in-experienced Emma. She wanted to be a woman who could rock his world. "I do want this. I want you. Let me take off your suit. I want you to take off my dress."

"I sense hesitation."

Blue light from the city filtered through the living room windows and pooled on the foyer floor. She looked deeply into his eyes. Even that much felt bold. It wasn't daylight, but she wasn't shying away. If she did nothing else right, let her confront him with this. Let her be honest and trust that he wouldn't think less of her. "I have to tell you something."

"Please." His voice rumbled with concern.

"I'm worried I might disappoint you."

He unleashed his off-kilter smile. He shook his head, tugging her closer and kissing her tenderly. First her lips, then her jaw, and finally—blissfully—her neck. "Nothing about you is disappointing."

Emma swallowed hard. Did he really feel that way? Was it the truth? Or had she merely done a good job of convincing him she was something she wasn't? His roving lips on her neck weren't helping her sort any of this out. "I've only been with one man, Daniel. Ever."

He reared back his head, vision narrowed. "Did your family actually lock you up in a tower somewhere? I don't see how dozens of men haven't at least tried to seduce you."

It was both surprising and oddly reassuring to know that Daniel saw her that way. "Not a tower. A small apartment. And my mother was especially good at keeping tabs on me."

"I know the feeling."

She sensed that he did. "I've never enjoyed myself with a man. I never reached my ultimate destination, if you get what I mean."

"Never?"

This conversation had already gone so much further than she'd intended. She should be feeling humiliated right now, but she wasn't. Something about Daniel made her want to be an open book. He made her want to bare her soul *and* her body. "Not with him."

He slid his hand down the back of her left arm, then locked his fingers with hers. "You've never had an orgasm?"

Heat flushed her face, but she refused to be embarrassed. "I have. Many times. By myself."

A knowing look crossed his face. "So you know what you like?"

"I think so. I'm sure there's a lot I've been missing out on, though."

He got serious again, the crease between his eyes deepening. "Emma, you couldn't disappoint me if you tried. Tonight has been incredible."

However much she'd wanted him a minute ago, that desire was tenfold now. She reached back and pulled the clip from her hair, letting her hair fall down onto her shoulders. Daniel sucked in a sharp breath and she knew she was not only on the right track, but this was the only way she wanted to go. She tightened her grip around his waist. "I want you to show me what I've been missing."

A lustful groan came from the depths of Daniel's throat. "I will." He slipped the thin strap from her shoulder. She shuddered with anticipation. He pressed a kiss to her bare skin, and she tilted her head to the side, silently begging him to kiss her neck again. Daniel claimed the stretch of skin with his mouth. His kisses were wet and hungry. Heat pooled between her legs. "Just do what feels right. Do what feels natural."

She anticipated no problem with that. Daniel was so sexy, her body was giving her hundreds of cues. Heat coursed through her veins. Her skin was alive with electricity. She turned her back to him and twisted her hair to the side. "I've heard you're good with zippers."

"I'm terrible. I can't promise you'll ever be able to wear this dress again."

She smiled as he unzipped her, his breath warm against the back of her neck. "That's okay. I've already been seen in it." Her pulse picked up when she realized that, unlike the other night, she was free to let her dress fall. He undid the tiny hook at the top and she pulled the garment from her shoulders, letting it flounce to the floor.

Daniel placed his hands on her hips and flattened himself against her back. She could already feel his erection, hard against her bottom. He smoothed his palms around to her belly, pulling her into him while he dragged his fingers up her torso. Her nipples drew tight just waiting for his touch.

He kissed her neck again. "It's so sexy that you didn't wear a bra tonight," he muttered into the sensitive spot behind her ear. He cupped her breasts with his sizable hands, enveloping them and squeezing.

She felt light-headed as pleasure and excitement had her heart racing again. "The dress did the dictating."

"Bravo for the dress." He rolled her nipples between his fingertips. Emma clamped her eyes shut, sinking back against his chest as currents zipped from her breasts to the tops of her thighs. He slid one hand down her midline and into the front of her panties. His fingers spread her delicate folds. "You're so wet." His breath was warm against her ear. He gently nipped her lobe.

"I want you," she gasped, as he found her apex and

began rubbing in small circles. He knew precisely what he was doing, his fingers driving her straight toward her peak. She felt it zeroing in on her, building so fast she could hardly think straight. "I'm going to come…"

The words had hardly left her lips before she knocked her head back and the orgasm slammed into her, hard. It felt so impossibly good, waves of blissful heat washing over her. Still she was a bit mortified that it hadn't taken much to bring her there. She turned in his arms, grabbed both sides of his head and brought his lips to hers, threading her fingers into his hair. "That was amazing. I'm sorry it happened so fast."

"Don't apologize. That's just the beginning." He reached down and scooped up her legs, lifting her into his arms. "Which way to your bed?"

She pointed to the hall and he strode to her bedroom, taking charge, every inch the confident man she was so immensely attracted to. She coiled her hands around his neck, still reeling from the pleasure he'd delivered. He ducked into the darkness of her room and placed her feet on the floor. Emma took both his hands and walked backward to the bed. Her calves met the mattress and she raced to start on his shirt. He caressed her bare shoulders while she freed the buttons, then pushed the crisp cotton down his arms. Being able to smooth her hands over his firm chest was the best reward. His muscles were hard and defined, even better than her brain had imagined. But there was more waiting for her, so she unhooked his belt, the hook and zipper on his trousers. They dropped to the floor and Daniel took her hand, pressing her palm against his erection. His body was telling her just how primed he was. She'd made him feel like that.

She pressed harder and he groaned, but she wanted to touch him for real, not just through his boxer briefs. Pure instinct taking over, she shimmied them down his hips and took him into her hand. She wanted to feel every inch of him. Her thumb smoothed over the head, silky smooth. Daniel groaned again. She slid her fingers along his length and began to stroke from base to tip, matching the tension coiling beneath his skin with her firm grip. He kissed her with abandon, mouth open and craving. He needed her. She felt it in every inch of him that she touched. She sensed it in every kiss and subtle moan.

The pressure was building between her legs again and she ached for him to touch her. She placed a knee on the bed and, wanting him to truly see her, stretched out on her back, her body on full display. She wanted him to see that she was his for the taking.

He reached down and curled his fingers into the waistband of her silky panties, tugged them down her legs and tossed them aside. She expected him to stretch out on the bed next to her, but he watched her instead. She squirmed against the sheets, rubbing her head back and forth. It felt like she was on fire.

"Do you have a condom?" she asked, kicking herself for not thinking this through and buying a box ahead of time.

"I do." He reached for his pants and opened his wallet. "A gentleman is always prepared."

Emma sat up, her heart racing. "Come here. Let me put it on."

He grinned and handed over the packet, standing between her knees. Their gazes connected as she rolled it on. Her fingers didn't fumble. It was like she was a different person. She felt him get harder in her hand. She'd never wanted anything as badly as she wanted Daniel. She lay back on the bed and spread her legs for him. He lowered his beautiful body onto her, positioning himself at her entrance and then slowly driving inside.

Emma raised her knees and he sank down until his hips met the back of her thighs. He felt so impossibly good, filling her completely. He lowered his torso against hers, resting on his elbows, but putting a delicious pressure against her center. His thrusts were pure magic, his hips rotating with every pass. She might not last long the second time, either. They fell into a kiss that had no logical end. Passionate. Unafraid. It was like they'd done this hundreds of times together, but the newness was there, too. It was a feeling unlike anything she'd ever experienced.

Daniel's breaths were getting shorter, his thrusts longer and deeper. He pushed back with one arm and lowered his head, drawing her nipple into his mouth. Emma wrapped her legs around him, muscling him closer. She felt like her entire body was about to burst. She was poised. Muscles tight and inching closer to release. And she gave way, ecstasy washing over her in a colorful array of light. Daniel followed, his torso freezing in place, deep moans coming from his incredible mouth. He took several more slow passes, his hips delivering aftershocks of pleasure to her.

As her heart rate slowed, he collapsed next to her, pulling her into his arms and kissing the top of her head over and over again. Emma was overcome with a powerful realization, one she hoped wasn't born of too much naive optimism. On paper, she and Daniel did not belong together. But alone, away from the rest of the world, they might be perfect.

Seven

Daniel woke to a feeling he hadn't given into for a very long time. He was daring to wonder what came next with a woman. Here in her bed, sheets tangled around them both, he wasn't thinking about any work he had to do today. He was instead wondering if they could go out to dinner. He was wondering if she might want to come over. He was at ease with her already, and she was more than comfortable with him. He'd loved every minute of seeing her open up to him physically last night. She'd picked up on his cues and given herself fully to him. He hadn't banked on the emotional side of that. He felt connected to her. Fast. Exactly what he'd feared.

He already knew he couldn't let his mother continue to believe he was trying to extract information about Eden's from Emma. The small bits he'd learned thus far would remain under lock and key. Still, he had to devote some time to thinking through how this might possibly work. Was there a happy middle ground? Or was he fooling himself because he was in bed with a beautiful woman?

Daniel's arm was pinned under Emma's shoulders, and he was starting to lose the feeling in his fingers. He carefully tried to unthread himself from her, but that was enough to make her stir.

"Are you awake?" she grumbled. "It's still early." Her morning voice was soft and velvety, just like her. She rolled over and faced him, settling her head on his chest. "You smell nice in the morning."

Such a funny and sweet thing to say. It made something in the vicinity of his heart swell. He shook his head, trailing his fingers up and down her back, bringing back memories of their night together and the ways they'd pleased each other. "You smell nice, too. I should get up, though. The dogs will surely want to get out."

Emma sat up, her wide eyes popping open. She didn't bother to cover herself, baring her luscious curves to him. "I can't believe we forgot."

How adorable was it that she'd used the word *we*?

"It's okay. I snuck upstairs after three to let them out and to grab some different clothes. They don't like it when I don't come home at night."

Emma arched her eyebrows and narrowed a skeptical stare at him. "Does that happen a lot?"

"Not at all in New York."

A wide smile bloomed on her face. She leaned down and kissed him on the cheek, then swatted his leg. "Good. Come on. I'll go with you." She hopped out of bed and traipsed over to her dresser, fishing out some clothes.

He was inclined to let the dogs wait a few more minutes just so he could enjoy watching her flit around the room naked. But he couldn't let responsibility get too far away from him. He was doing enough of that already. "You don't have to come with me if you'd rather sleep."

Emma tugged on a pair of black leggings and a white tank top. "I love your dogs. I like being around them." She zipped up a gray hoodie. "I like being around you."

"I like being around you, too." Again, Daniel was wading in deeper. The depth didn't scare him so much as his own enthusiasm for going there.

When they arrived upstairs, the dogs were raring to go, especially Jolly, who was running in circles. Emma got her on her leash while Daniel took care of Buck and Mandy. Minutes later, they arrived in the park. Emma took his hand and he led the way on the loop the dogs preferred. He was struck by how this was all so normal. So calm. Of course, things might change when they ended their walk at the newsstand. Daniel cringed at the thought of what the papers might say. Hopefully, there had been more interesting tabloid fodder in attendance last night.

They came to a stop so the dogs could mark some

bushes. Jolly was sticking to Emma's side. "She likes you a lot. A lot more than she likes me."

"She doesn't realize that you made a sacrifice by adopting her. She's probably still waiting for your brother to come back."

He wondered if that was true. "Probably. I think my mother's wondering the same thing."

"What happened? When he died? It clearly caused some problems in your family. I can hear it in your voice."

Daniel cleared his throat. He'd never had his chance to tell his side of the story. He'd kept it all bottled up inside for two years. "William and I had an argument the night he got into the accident. I was quite angry and told him that he was no longer my brother."

Emma held her hand to her lips. "Wow. What made you say that?"

"He was having an affair with my fiancée, Bea, and I found out about it. We'd always competed with each other and they'd dated once or twice before she and I started going out. I don't know if she just liked the idea of playing us off against each other or what, but that's what happened. So those were the last words I said to my brother. My mother never forgave me. She's convinced that William wouldn't have crashed if he hadn't been so upset."

Emma shook her head. "No. I'm sure that's not what happened. And of course you were upset. Your brother betrayed you."

"But there's no winning that argument. He's gone now. I will always have regrets."

Emma scooped up Jolly and looked her right in the face. "You and your dad need to get things worked out. You both miss the same person."

Daniel smiled. She was truly amazing. Just then, his cell phone rang. He pulled it from his pocket. The caller ID said it was Charlotte Locke, his real estate agent. He wasn't sure he should take this call with Emma nearby.

Emma put Jolly back down on the ground. "It's okay if you need to answer your phone."

"It'll just be a moment. I'm so sorry." Daniel handed her the leashes and distanced himself. "Hello?"

"Daniel. It's Charlotte. Do you have a minute? We need to talk."

Daniel watched Emma with the dogs. They were already hopelessly head over heels for her. Mandy and Buck were practically climbing over each other to get to her, while Jolly circled her ankles. Their tails wagged with endless excitement. "Of course. News on the lease?"

"I'm afraid not. I'm not going to be able to work with you any longer."

"What? We're in the middle of a negotiation." Daniel couldn't believe this. Charlotte was one of the top agents in the city and he'd still come up empty-handed. He'd never get Stone's off the ground with someone else. "Why now?"

"A long-time client has asked me to stop working with you."

"Excuse me?"

"I'm sorry. I can't explain further."

"Can you tell me who the client is?"

"I'm sorry. No."

Daniel was reeling. Who would cut him off at the knees like this? As he eyed Emma, he couldn't help but suspect this could be connected to Eden's. The conclusion made his stomach lurch, but the history between their families made sabotage likely. "Can you at least refer me to someone else? You told me you have a great relationship with this landlord."

Charlotte cleared her throat. "I do. And I'm sorry, but I can't. But you have plenty of resources, Mr. Stone. I have no doubt that you'll land on your feet. Have a good day." Before Daniel could utter another word, Charlotte had hung up.

Daniel jammed his cell phone into his pocket. His blood was on the brink of boiling. If he were in London or Paris right now, he'd have no problem finding a new agent. Now he was starting over from scratch.

"Everything okay? You look terrible." Emma approached, the dogs not so much leading the way as staying by her side.

It was such a shame. He liked Emma a great deal, but the suspicions going through his head right now were exactly why he had no business becoming involved with her. When he was younger and felt indestructible, he would've thumbed his nose at his gut feelings. He'd ignored the signs with William and Bea and it had destroyed his world. "Actually, everything isn't okay. It appears my real estate agent has left me. I'm wondering if you know anything about this."

"How could I?"

"Then perhaps your sisters?"

"You think they got your agent to dump you? They would never do something like that." Her eyebrows popped up as a realization crossed her face. "So you really are opening a Stone's in New York. This isn't early days or you just exploring your options. You're doing this."

"You had to know that. I don't for a minute believe you are naive enough to think I'm spending time in New York looking at real estate for anything else."

Emma reared her head back. Jolly growled at him. "Wow." She shook her head slowly, looking him square in the eye. "You could have just been up front with me. You hedged your answer and I took you at your word. Now I'm thinking that was a foolish move on my part."

Daniel's anger was quickly replaced by guilt. He'd skirted the issue when asked. That much was true. "I thought we were toying with each other."

Emma shook her head. "I don't play games, Daniel. Maybe other women have done that to you, but not me. Maybe your old fiancée did that to you, but that's just not my style." Emma collected the dog leashes and placed them in his hand. Her touch sent an ache right through him. She began to walk away.

"Where are you going?"

She turned around, walking backward. "To talk to my sisters. If you're right, this has to stop now."

"And if I'm wrong?"

"It won't be the first time you've had to apologize to me."

Emma called Sophie as soon as she was back in her apartment. No answer. Next, Mindy. Voice mail. What in the world was going on? Had those two really resorted to cutting Daniel off at the knees? She'd told him they wouldn't do such a thing, but she worried she might be wrong. She had to get to the office right away to track down her sisters.

She got into the shower. "This is so stupid," she muttered to herself. "What kind of families feud with each other?" She placed a foot on the stone ledge meant for shaving her legs and aggressively scrubbed, suds splatting against the glass walls of the shower enclosure. "It's not like we're the Montagues and they're the Capulets. We're not even the Hatfields and the McCoys. If we're fighting, we're talking about who might sell the most perfume and designer shoes. Why does anybody need dirty tricks to do that?"

She shut off the water, stepped onto the plush bathmat and wrapped herself up in a fluffy towel. Swiping at the fog on the mirror with her hand, she looked at herself. If what Daniel had accused her sisters of was true, this was worse than stupid. It couldn't continue. It didn't matter how much money was on the line, she wasn't about to be a part of underhanded tactics.

And then it hit her—what if it wasn't true? What

did Daniel's assumption say about him? It certainly demanded that she look at last night through a different lens. But she didn't want to do that. It had been too amazing. She wouldn't let circumstance color her view of something she'd enjoyed so much.

Her phone buzzed with a text. She flipped it over on the bathroom counter. The message was from Duane, head of store security for Eden's.

Customers lined up for the dress you wore last night. Have Gregory text me when you arrive.

She did a quick search on her phone. Sure enough, she and Daniel had hit the tabloids again.

An Eden Princess and Her Enemy Prince.

There was that word again, the one she hated so much—*enemy*. The story focused on the hatred between the families and the businesses, and how unlikely a pair Daniel and Emma were. The reporter surmised it would never last. Emma knew the odds were stacked against them, but she at least wanted her chance. She and Daniel looked nothing but right in the pictures, holding hands on the red carpet, smiling at each other. Daniel was so handsome it made her entire body tingle, especially when she thought about the things they'd done together in bed. That was the happy ending she'd wanted, not the nightmare of the last half hour.

When Emma arrived at Eden's, there were twice as many photographers outside as last time. Duane had them cordoned off to one side of the store entrance with the sort of metal barricades the city put up for parades. Meanwhile, customers were standing in an orderly line marked off by velvet ropes and brass stanchions—a line that went all the way to the corner of the block and wrapped around the building.

"Wow," Emma said. "Looks like we're selling some dresses today." This was a better reaction than she'd hoped for. The public didn't care about family feuds. Why should anyone else? If there was any evidence that Mindy and Sophie should be listening to her, this was it.

Her driver, Gregory, glanced back over his shoulder. "Duane wants us to wait until he can escort you to the door."

"I see him." Emma opened her own door and all hell broke loose.

The photographers ran out from behind the metal barricade and descended on her. They weren't asking questions, just setting off flashbulbs in her face, while the people in line shouted her name. *Emma! Emma!* Duane got to her at the same time Gregory did, and the two men shielded her, rushing her to the door. Gregory dropped back and Duane followed her inside.

"This is crazy." Emma neatened her hair and headed straight for the elevators. "I want us to sell dresses, but this seems a bit much."

Duane was breathing hard. "People love a budding romance."

Romance. Duane was capable of focusing on the positive. Why wasn't everyone else? "Thank you for dealing with all of that. No big media events for me for a while. Hopefully, things will go back to normal." She stepped onto the elevator.

Upstairs, the offices were exactly that—normal. It was like any other day. Lizzie was on the phone, writing something down. She gave Emma a quick wave. Down the hall, Mindy's office door was closed, her light off. She often arrived late, so that was no big surprise. Ever the workaholic, Sophie had her door open and her desk a verifiable mess, but she was on a call, her back turned away. Emma dropped her things in her own office and waited patiently for Sophie to finish.

"Knock, knock." Emma rapped on the door frame. "Do you have a minute?"

Sophie looked up. "Well, if it isn't Princess Emma." She waved the newspaper in the air, then handed it over. "Nora Bradford's office called. They're pleased. In fact, they're agreeing to our terms for the new five-year license. I just need you to work out a few points on the financial side and get them to sign off on everything."

Emma was welling with pride. This was a big development. "Oh, fantastic. I'm happy to take things over from here."

"I have to say thank-you. Nora was so happy I think I convinced her to not only design my wedding gown, but the bridesmaids' dresses, as well."

"Oh, wow. That's amazing."

Sophie stuffed some papers into a folder. "It really is. I'd been unable to pull that off on my own."

"Nice job with the press, Ems." Mindy's voice came from the doorway. For once, it wasn't full of ire.

"I'm thinking we should get you to host a celebrity pop-up in the store," Sophie said to Emma.

"Great idea," Mindy said. "Ooh. Yes. Next week. I don't think we should wait."

"You want me to host a pop-up?" Emma had attended only one of these events, where Eden's asked a notable person in fashion or pop culture to curate a collection of favorite items from the store for an exclusive invite-only shopping night. Only Eden's biggest spenders would be in attendance.

"Yes, you. Like Mindy said, we should strike while the iron is hot," Sophie said.

"Uh. Okay. Fine." Emma officially no longer knew what was going on in her world.

"Speaking of hot, we need to talk about Daniel Stone," Mindy said. "A date so you can show off a Nora Bradford dress is one thing, but you cannot be dating him for real. He's going to chew you up and spit you out."

"She's right," Sophie added. "Plus, things will get really awkward once we start discussing strategy to squash Stone's New York."

Emma's stomach sank. Was Daniel right? "Did you guys get Charlotte Locke to drop Daniel as a client?"

"What? What happened?" Sophie asked.

"Daniel was dropped by Charlotte Locke. So now he's starting from scratch with looking for a location for Stone's. He thinks we were involved."

Sophie pursed her lips. "If we were going to interfere, that would have been the logical place to start."

"So you didn't do it?"

Sophie pressed her hand to her chest. "Not me. Mindy? Anything you need to tell us?"

Mindy shook her head. "No way. I'm fine with Stone's moving into New York. If they want to compete with us, let them try. At least it might make things interesting around here."

Emma rubbed her forehead, playing mental catch-up. She had no idea who had sabotaged Daniel, but it wasn't her or her sisters. That was all that mattered right now. "Sophie, is there any way you can do me a favor? Can you reach out to Charlotte and see if she'll reconsider? Just in the interest of good sportsmanship?"

"You want us to help him?" Sophie's voice was incredulous. "No way. Not a Stone."

"Just as a sign of goodwill. That we're willing to fight fair."

Sophie planted her elbow on the desk and her chin on her hand, looking over at Mindy. "Thoughts?"

"We don't want the papers thinking we sabotaged him. But we still need to talk about Emma and Daniel." Mindy cast a stern look at Emma. "Are you going to keep seeing him?"

"I'd like to."

Mindy closed her eyes and shook her head. The implication was that Emma couldn't possibly be any stupider. "You do realize there are other men in the city, right?"

"I know. But I like him. A lot. We get along great. We had an amazing night last night."

"Did you sleep with him?" Sophie asked, her voice reaching a superhigh pitch.

"Have you seen him?" Mindy interjected. "Of course she did." She turned to Emma, her eyebrows drawing together in concern. "Please tell me you at least had sex with him."

Heat flushed Emma's face. Memories of last night flooded her mind, every last one white-hot and unforgettable. "I did."

"Oh, boy," Sophie said, making it sound as if Emma was a lost cause.

"It was just one night." Except that it was so much more. She knew that the instant she'd tried to be dismissive. They'd made a connection last night, one she was inclined to fight for, even with outside forces trying to push them apart. "If you could just make that phone call, Sophie, that would be great. I'd like to at least be able to tell Daniel that we never set out to screw him over."

As soon as Emma left, Sophie called Jake to have him fix the Charlotte Locke situation. "Everything should be back to normal very soon," Sophie said to Mindy when she hung up the phone.

"I'm worried about Emma."

"Me, too." Sophie tapped her fingers on her desk. She did so whenever she was feeling uncertain. She said it helped her focus. Right now, it was making Mindy even more upset. Sophie's ten-carat Fred Leighton engagement ring glimmered, a reminder that Sophie had the world at her feet right now—her dream job and her dream guy, Jake Wheeler, a man as rich as he was handsome, funny and charming to boot. Come October, they would be married.

And now Emma was taking center stage with splashy headlines dubbing her Princess Emma, while she seemed to be pursuing the impossible—a romance with a member of the Stone family. Meanwhile, Mindy herself was in perpetual limbo, professionally and personally. She spent her days trying to perform her duties at Eden's while keeping her own company afloat. And as for her guy, Sam was more a pipe dream than a dream come true. Sam was not a man you pinned down. He was always the one doing the pinning.

Mindy crossed her legs, bobbing her foot so forcefully that her Christian Louboutin pump popped free from her heel and dangled on her toes. There was too much pent-up frustration coursing through her body right now. Her mind flew to Sam, the man who had no problem helping her unwind. She desperately wished he was in town. No matter his commitment to business, he always made himself available for a midday tryst. "I realize Emma has done some good things for the store, but I'm sure this Daniel Stone thing is going to blow up in our faces. She's so impressionable and you know she's caught up in the excitement of being in the papers. I can totally see her falling for the handsome guy and selling us down the river."

"I'm worried, too, but what are we supposed to do? We have to believe she's on our side."

"Why?"

"She has a fortune tied up in being on our side."

Mindy shook her head, unconvinced. "She knows what it's like to have nothing. That scares the crap out of me."

"Are you listening to yourself? She came from nothing. She's not going to throw this away. And you agreed with her that there's no reason for us to interfere with Stone's. They think they can move in on our home turf and beat us at our game? Let them try."

"I worry she's too naive. Daniel will deceive her and we'll have to pick up the pieces of our business *and* her heart."

Sophie pressed her lips together. "I think she's doing her best in a tough situation. She likes him. She feels she can keep work and fun separate. We have to trust her. We can't tell a grown woman what to do with her personal life." On the desk, Sophie's cell phone buzzed with a text. She turned it over and a goofy smile crossed her lips. "Oh. Jake's here. We're going to look at a few possible wedding locations." She leaped from her chair and opened her office door.

Jake walked in, looking as ridiculously handsome as ever in a killer suit. He came bearing a gift, too—a fragrant bouquet of bright pink flowers. "Hello, gorgeous." He placed a soft kiss on Sophie's lips.

"Peonies. You shouldn't have."

"I wanted to."

"They're beautiful." Sophie beamed like the smitten bride-to-be. Mindy had always looked forward to the day her sister would get married, but as the oldest, she'd assumed it would be her turn first. "I'll get these to Lizzie so she can put them in some water."

Jake grinned as he watched Sophie walk away. "Hey, Mindy." He strolled over and leaned down, pecking her on the cheek.

"Thank you for straightening out the Charlotte Locke situation."

"I still don't know who got to her, but things are back to normal for Daniel Stone. You could have left him flapping in the wind, you know. Someone with pockets that deep will find a new agent."

"I know. But it's the principle of the thing. We don't want it to look like we'd play dirty pool." Only members of the Stone family employed such low-down, backhanded tactics. The Eden family remained far above the fray. "Plus, we're trying to keep Emma happy. She and Daniel Stone are quite the item."

Jake nodded. "So I saw in the tabloids."

Sophie reappeared in the doorway. "Ready?" she asked Jake.

"Always," he answered.

"See you later?" Sophie asked Mindy.

"Of course." She watched as her sister and Jake wandered down the hall. Sometimes, it looked like they were walking on air.

Mindy's stomach was an anxious tangle right now, and Jake's mention of not knowing who had prompted Charlotte Locke to make her move was eating at her. Why did she find herself wondering whether it might have been Sam? Probably because he was not an Eden, and if anyone was known for stooping to low levels, it was him. This certainly had the hallmark of a Sam move, but it didn't make sense. His aim had always been taking down Eden's, not propping it up. Her only course of action was asking him straight up if he had anything to do with it.

She crossed the hall to her office to grab her prized gray Birkin bag. She had to stop by the By Min-vitation Only office, and with Sophie away for a bit, this was her best window of opportunity. Plus, she preferred that her visits be unannounced. Her interim CEO, Matthew Hawkins, seemed to have a real talent for doing whatever he wanted to do, regardless of any precedent set by Mindy. The last time she'd dropped by, he had them completely reworking one of the production lines. She couldn't let Hawkins put his stamp on her business. It was still her ship to steer.

"I'm heading over to the BMO office," she said to Lizzie, breezing past her desk. She pressed the elevator button and studied their irreplaceable receptionist as she juggled a call, signed for a delivery and arranged Sophie's flowers. As soon as she hung up the phone, Mindy had to ask, "Lizzie, when was the last time you got a raise?"

She blew her spiky bangs from her forehead. "It's been more than a year. My last performance review was supposed to happen the day after your grandmother passed away. It sort of fell between the cracks."

Mindy was horrified. "You're kidding."

Lizzie shook her head. "It's totally understandable. We were all in shock when she died, and Sophie was more than a little busy then. It's not a big deal."

The elevator arrived and Mindy held it. "First thing I'm doing after I get back from lunch is fixing that. You're too valuable to be treated like that. I'm so sorry that happened."

Lizzie smiled, but it was more relief than happiness. "Thank you so much. I'll see you when you get back, Ms. Eden."

Out on the street, Mindy donned her Chloé sunglasses and greeted her driver, who opened the Escalade door for her. She pulled out her phone and looked at the time. If she was going to confront Sam, this was the time to do it, away from the microscope of Eden's. She pulled up his name on speed dial. He answered after only one ring.

"This is a sexy surprise," he said.

Damn him. Everything about him—his voice, his words—made her weak. He always knew how to make her smile, how to bring her to her knees. "Do you have a minute? I need to ask you a question."

"I always have a minute for you."

"Where are you, anyway?"

"London. I have a meeting, then I'm on to Frankfurt and Prague."

"Big deals in the works?"

"I hope so. I'm investing enough time and money in them. Just some real estate. A possible tech acquisition." Sam didn't worry about carving out a niche. It was more about having a nose for profit.

"Speaking of real estate, do you know Charlotte Locke?"

"Of course. I know all three Locke siblings."

"Do you know anything about Daniel Stone? Because Charlotte was his real estate agent until she dumped him early this morning, and everyone thinks Sophie and I were behind it."

"Are you calling to share this bit of news, or are you calling because you think I did it? Because I did."

Her hunch had been correct. Mindy blew out a breath and shook her head. "Great. This puts me in a terrible position. You know that, right?"

"I never want you in a bad position. I only want you in the best possible ones. Preferably ones with a good view." Everything Sam said somehow led back to sex. When she wasn't angry with him, she liked it quite a lot.

"I don't understand why you would do that. You're the one who's always scheming for the demise of Eden's. Why go after our competition?"

"Have you really not figured out what motivates me, Mindy?"

"Aside from money and sex, no. I haven't figured you out. At all."

"I want what you want. You told me you felt trapped by Eden's, so I thought of ways for you to get out. You told me you were committed to succeeding with your sisters, so I did what I had to do to take your competitor out of the way. It's very simple, Mindy. I just want you happy."

"I don't believe you. You always think about yourself first."

"It's not my job to convince you. But it's the truth."

Her mind was running a million miles a minute. Was that really true? Did he actually care? Most of the time, he seemed so blasé about everything, especially her. It wasn't like Mindy to make demands, but something told her it was time to put everything on the line. She did not want to keep sitting idly by, letting her heart be subject to the whims of a man she wanted badly. "If you want me happy, you won't go to Frankfurt or Prague."

"Where would you like me to go instead?"

"Come back to New York. And when you get here, come straight to my apartment. Even if it's the middle of the night." Her heart was pounding like a bass drum, not knowing how he would react.

"And how long am I staying?"

Mindy gnawed on her fingernail. It was time to ask for everything she wanted. "Until I figure out what in the world I should do with you."

Eight

Daniel was just as shocked by Charlotte Locke's second phone call that day as he'd been by the first.

"We're still full speed ahead with the lease negotiation?" He tapped a pen on the mahogany desk in his home office.

"Yes. I should know something in a few days. There are quite a few layers of bureaucracy with the property management company. And I'm sorry about the confusion earlier today. My other client is, well…" Charlotte hesitated, as if she felt the need to parse her words. "I'll say they're particular. And not easy to please. I hope you can understand that I had to show loyalty. There's a lot of family history mixed in. It makes everything more complicated."

If ever there was a situation Daniel could relate

to, it was one where family history made everything hopelessly tricky. He only hoped that Emma wasn't somehow involved. "I'm glad to be back on track."

Daniel said goodbye to Charlotte and got off the call. He waited for some sense of relief to settle in, but it showed no signs of coming. He was just as torn up and conflicted as he'd felt that morning. His conversation with Emma was still fresh in his mind. She'd insisted that she didn't play games. That was a refreshing idea. If it proved to be true.

His phone rang again and he was dismayed to see it was his mother. Luckily, he hadn't had to tell her about losing his agent for a few hours. "Hello, Mum," he said.

"Hello. Have we got an update on finding a space?"

He hadn't told his mother about the lease, since she would only give him a hard time if he began negotiations and they failed. But it would be nice to deliver good news for once. "I do, actually. I just got off the phone with the agent. Lease negotiations are under way. We should know something next week if all goes well."

His mother let out a squeal on the other end of the line. "Wonderful. Simply wonderful. Which one is it? The last one you sent pictures of?"

"That's the one."

"Oh, good. It's perfect. Only five blocks from Eden's. I'd like to be able to go head-to-head with them."

"That's not why I chose it. The architecture of

the building is lovely. It needs some work, but it has enough history that it will make sense for the store."

"Well, I'm glad we're moving forward. Now what's the latest with Nora Bradford?"

Daniel cleared his throat, his stomach uneasy. No matter what might happen between Emma and him, he wasn't sure he was cutthroat enough to steal a designer from Eden's. "I've been wondering if we shouldn't go in a different direction. Perhaps focus on some new up-and-coming designers. Someone fresh and exciting who we can get for a good price."

"I saw the papers, Daniel. Miriam in my office showed them to me. You're still seeing that woman and she's still wearing Nora Bradford dresses for all the world to see."

"Emma and I went to the opera. I told you we've developed a friendship. It's nothing more serious than that. Trust me, I know what I'm doing."

"I don't like wondering where my own son's loyalty lies."

Oh, how Daniel could have turned the tables on her. She'd shown so much more loyalty to William than she'd shown to him. She'd simply refused to believe the stories about William and Bea. "You don't have to worry."

Of course, Daniel was nothing but worried right now. He felt as though he was teetering atop a house of cards.

"I want Nora Bradford. If you won't get her, I will."

"I'll work on it, okay? I'm also going to send you information about some other choices. Designers that will still bring customers into the store. In the end, that's all that matters."

"Fine. I'll look at them, but I don't want to play around."

"Neither do I."

Daniel got off the phone and ran his hands through his hair. The sooner he could get his mother to retire, the happier he would be. The question was when? Not any time in the immediate future, he feared.

A knock came at the door and Jolly tore off, barking like crazy. Mandy and Buck were close behind. "Shush!" he snapped. Jolly quickly obeyed the order, although she looked as though she resented it greatly.

He took a peek through the hole in the door. There through the fish-eye was Emma. The universe did not make a habit of sending him happy things, and he knew he shouldn't be having this reaction, but there was a smile a mile wide across his face. He opened the door.

"Emma. This is…" He watched as she crouched down and Jolly hopped up and down on her stubby rear legs, tail wagging.

Emma looked up at him, her eyes like a beacon in the middle of a dark night. "What? A surprise?" She straightened back to standing.

"I hate to be so unoriginal, but yes."

"I came to tell you that neither of my sisters had anything to do with Charlotte dropping you. Have you heard from her? Sophie made a phone call to try and sort things out."

So he had been wrong. So very wrong. He reached

for her arm, his pulse pounding. "She did call me. All has been fixed. I'm so sorry I assumed you or your sisters might be involved. I jumped ahead and I shouldn't have done that without more information. I hope you'll accept my apology."

"I do. Of course I do."

He was still so in awe of her generous nature. "Thank you."

"I have to be honest. I wasn't entirely certain that my sisters hadn't done it. I'm still learning to trust them. It's not easy. And this whole thing about the feud between our families? Is it just me or is it a little crazy?"

Daniel smiled. How they could be of the same mind so often, he didn't know. "I agree. In this day and age, it simply doesn't make sense."

"I guess that's what happens when there's so much money on the line, huh?"

"And pride. Don't forget about that."

Emma nodded in agreement. "So I think the question is, what do we want to do about it?"

"In terms of business?"

She shook her head. "No, Daniel. In terms of us. I like you. I like you a lot. And it's more than just last night, although last night was spectacular..." Her voice trailed off and Daniel watched as color rose in her cheeks. She was thinking about him the same way he'd been thinking about her. He was sure of it.

He took her hand and pulled her closer. "Last night was unbelievable. I hate the idea that we'd only get to do those things once." He could feel his own body temperature spiking. Every nerve ending was crackling with electricity.

"I agree. I totally agree. Can we find a way to put everyone else's baggage off to the side? It doesn't seem fair to either of us."

It seemed an impossible task. Daniel's entire life revolved around his business and his family, but he knew the same was true for her. Maybe they could do this. He wanted to try. "Agreed." He realized there was another component to their short relationship that wasn't working, at least not for him. "I have a request of my own to make, though. Can we please stay away from the press?"

"The hubbub about Eden's starting to get to you?"

"Honestly, no. I know how hard it is to come by a boon like that. You find a means of creating excitement and you seize it."

"So then what is it?"

"What has been in the newspaper twice will quickly become five times, then ten. Then we'll reach the point where even taking the dogs across the street will become an ordeal. We'll be living in a fishbowl, and trust me, it's no way to live."

"That's what you were trying to tell me last night, before the opera, isn't it? Was this after your brother's accident?"

"It was." Daniel's nightmarish memories sprang to life again, of trying to outrun reporters and photographers on the streets in London while they shouted questions at him about William and Bea. He didn't want to think about those things now, not when he had

Emma here. "I don't want to talk about it. Not now. Not while I have the chance to kiss you."

He placed his hand on her hip and slid it around to the small of her back. He was prepared to pull her forward, but he didn't have to do a thing. Before he had the chance to think, Emma had dropped her handbag on the floor and threaded her hands into his hair. She kissed him eagerly, backing him up until his spine met the wall.

"Is it bad if I say I've been thinking about this non-stop since last night?" Emma yanked his shirt out of the waistband of his jeans. Her fingers scrambled to undo the buttons.

"Not at all. I'd be lying if I said I hadn't been thinking about the same exact thing." Jolly yipped at Daniel's feet. "Somebody's jealous."

Emma leaned into Daniel and kissed him. "Is there somewhere we can be alone?"

"Absolutely." He took her hand and led her down the hall to his bedroom, closing the door behind them.

She perched on the edge of his bed, bouncing once or twice. "Nice." She was a vision too sexy and beautiful to believe. In a silvery-gray silk blouse and form-fitting black skirt, she was sheer sophistication with an edge. Exactly what he liked.

She reached down and pulled a sleek black pump from her foot, placing it on the floor. She did the same with the other. How he enjoyed watching, and waiting to see what she did next.

"Well?" she asked, popping the top button of her blouse and trailing her fingers down the edge of the placket. Her knuckles grazed the top of her breast. A growl worked its way through his throat. He wouldn't have thought it possible, but he wanted her more now than he had last night. He approached her and stood between her legs, letting her finish getting rid of his shirt. She smoothed her slender fingers across his abs. The admiration on her face was a great reward for all the hours he spent in the gym.

She looked up at him, seeming uncertain, as if she was waiting for him to tell her what she should do next. "You're thinking," he said. "Don't think too much. Just do what you want to." With a reassuring nod, he encouraged her.

She kissed his stomach, dragging her tongue across his skin as she unbuttoned his pants and pulled them down his legs. He dug his fingers into her silky hair, gently curling them into her scalp.

The tension in his hips was growing, the ache for her making him restless. He wanted to be in her hand, her mouth, inside her. As if she knew what he was thinking, she tugged his boxer briefs down and took his erection into her palm. She wrapped her fingers around him and he felt himself get harder with just that single touch. Then she lowered her head and took just the tip into her mouth, rolling her tongue over the smooth skin. Daniel's mind went blank. Rational thought was gone as she took him between her lips, sucking and licking. He touched her shoulders, the fabric of her blouse soft and sensuous against his hands, but what he really wanted was her naked. He leaned down and kissed the top of her head, urging her to let go of him.

She parted her lips with a pop and peered up at him. "Did I do something wrong?"

"You did everything right. Now I want to get you out of that blouse. And that skirt. And everything else."

Emma stood so Daniel could undress her. "Sure you don't want me to help?" she asked.

He shook his head, as he busied himself with unbuttoning her blouse. "No. This is the fun part."

"*This* is the fun part?"

He laughed. She really loved that sound. It even came out with a tinge of his wonderful accent. "It's the fun before the real fun."

He undid the final button and slipped his hands under the fabric and onto her shoulders. Just that one touch made her ready to give in. She dropped her head to one side as he dragged the sleeves down her arms. Then he dropped to his knees before her, and tugged her skirt and panties down in a single motion. Goose bumps dotted her skin when he looked up at her, and his blue eyes somehow darkened.

He smoothed both his hands over the upper part of her inner thighs, and with his fingertips, spread her wider. He lowered his head, and before Emma knew what was happening, he was pleasuring her with his tongue, rolling it in delicate circles over her apex. She clamped her eyes shut, quieting her mind and letting her body take over. It felt so good, and she willingly gave in to the heavenly sensations.

Once again her peak was barreling toward her. Perhaps it was just being with Daniel that had her so sensitized to his touch. Hot tension sizzled up her thighs. She took one hand and threaded her fingers into his hair, while with the other caressing her own breast through the lacy fabric of her bra, her nipple already tight from everything Daniel had aroused in her. The orgasm rolled over her slowly this time, growing in intensity, and Daniel followed the cues of her moans, changing his speed, playing her body like he was a master musician and she was his instrument.

Daniel sat back and looked up at her, grinning like he was pleased with himself. He had no idea. She dropped to her knees and kissed him with abandon, wrapping her fingers around his erection and stroking firmly.

"I need you now, Daniel. I'm not done yet."

He lunged for the bedside table drawer and pulled out a condom, quickly rolling it on. Emma kissed him again, hungrily, and urged him to his back, right there on the bedroom floor. She straddled his hips and lowered herself onto his body. Again, she was overwhelmed with how perfectly he filled her. How well they fitted together. She rocked back and forth as Daniel moved his hips. She liked how connected they were right now. It was like they were one.

Emma realized she still hadn't taken off her bra, so she reached back and unhooked it. Daniel's hands immediately went to her breasts, plucking at her nipples, bringing her back up to speed.

"I love this view of you," he said.

"I love *all* views of *you*."

He smiled and dragged one of his hands from her breast, down her midline, and settled his thumb against her apex. The man did not neglect this one part of a woman's body and she was so happy for it. He knew exactly how to make her feel her absolute best, sexy and adored all at the same time. She sat back a bit, resting her palms on his thighs and lifting her body higher with each pass. This gave Daniel an even more effective angle with his hand, and he brought her right to the brink.

His eyes were closed now, his mouth open, head to the side, breaths choppy. He was so handsome, she just had to watch, and the expressions on his face gave her enough clues to know when he was about to give way. She held tight, waiting for him, and when he began to squint, she let go. They both came at the same time, and that was an experience even better than she'd ever imagined. Colors and music swirled in her head while the ecstasy rushed through her body, every inch of it from her toes to the top of her skull. She pitched forward and collapsed on his chest, letting her full body weight rest on him.

He wrapped his arms around her and they kissed. And kissed again.

"That was unbelievable," she said.

"It was. Nothing like some floor sex to remind you you're alive." He took a playful nip of her neck.

"Very funny."

"But seriously. Let's get up into bed."

She climbed in under his fluffy duvet and he joined her after a quick trip to the bathroom. "I really am sorry I ever doubted you." His hand traced up and down her hip, soft and sensuous. He was so gentle when he wanted to be, and so commanding if that was his mood.

"It's okay, Daniel. Really." She cupped her fingers around his shoulder, feeling every hard contour. "There's a lot of bad blood between our families. It makes perfect sense that you would suspect my sisters. I just need you to know that it wouldn't be me."

A smile bloomed on his face and he rolled to his back. Emma smoothed her hand over his firm chest. "I do know that. My gut was telling me it couldn't have been you."

She cozied up next to him. It meant so much to have someone see the good in her. Many days, she felt invisible to the two people whose opinion she cared about most—Mindy and Sophie. But Daniel was stepping into the arena. She cared what he thought of her, and how he saw her. "I knew you were a good guy, Daniel. That's why I wanted so badly to be able to prove you wrong. I think it's time for us to turn our backs on this silly feud between Stone's and Eden's."

"Is there an opt-out form I missed?"

She playfully swatted his arm and leaned over to kiss him softly. "No. I'm just saying that we can say we won't play those sorts of games. We're the newest generation of both businesses, right? I want to find a way to get past the negativity. I don't see the point in it."

A deep crease formed between his eyes. He seemed leery at best. "Have any ideas how to do that?"

"We focus on the good. We focus on helping each other."

"You really think your sisters and my mother will be okay with that?"

"I'm not saying I'm going to come work for you or anything. But if it's the context of us dating, is anyone entitled to their opinion?" She quickly realized what she'd just said. "I'm sorry. I... I don't want to assume. This is only if you want to be dating."

He laughed quietly. "After the last few days, I don't want to be *not* dating you. Let's put it that way."

Her cheeks puffed up with a smile so fast it made her face hurt. "Good. Because I have an idea of how we can keep tearing down these walls."

"Tell me. Please."

"I have to host an evening shopping event at Eden's. I want you to be my date. Hold my hand and don't let me be nervous. Just like that night at Empire State."

"And you think your sisters will be okay with this?"

"As far as I'm concerned, they have to be. What choice do they have? Are they going to tell me I can't date you? A woman makes her own choices." There were more words about to spill out of her mouth. Did she have the nerve to say them? Something told her that she could make this leap with Daniel and it would pay off. She'd never felt this confident with a man before. It was exhilarating. "And I choose you."

From behind the door, there was a small bark. "Jolly," he said.

"Let her in."

"You sure? She might try to chase me out of bed."

Emma tossed back the comforter and tiptoed around the bed to the door, letting the dog in. She scooped up Jolly and climbed back under the covers next to Daniel. "It's time you two made some strides forward in your relationship."

Daniel narrowed his stare, full of skepticism. "I'm not going to talk about my feelings with her, if that's what you're suggesting."

Emma shook her head. She'd seen this advice on one of those reality shows about people who train difficult dogs. "It's a trust thing. She needs to see that I like you." She gave Jolly a scratch behind the ear, then leaned closer to Daniel and kissed his cheek.

"That's it?"

"It'll take time." She did it again. And again. Eventually, Jolly curled up between them and got comfortable.

"Now we have a dog between us, which is putting a serious damper on my plans for the rest of the night."

"The floor is always available. Or my place."

"Either one. Both. Whatever you want." His eyes scanned her face. How she could feel both exposed and comfortable at the same time, she wasn't sure.

"You're amazing. You know that, right?" he added.

She smiled and kissed him again, relishing the contentment that came when Daniel was being sweet. "You're the one who's amazing. I'm just being me."

Nine

Five days. Emma and Daniel had enjoyed five magnificent days together. No drama. No problems. Not even any gossip in the tabloids. Just five days of spending every nonworking moment together. A lot of their time had been spent in bed, but they'd done other things, like go out to dinner, and of course, they took many long walks in the park.

They switched back and forth between her place and his, but they spent each night together. Jolly still refused to give them much privacy, but she was being more consistently sweet to Daniel. Progress. Emma made a point of kissing him every time the dog was around. It seemed to be helping.

Emma had to wonder if things could really be this simple between her and Daniel. Had it been as easy as deciding they didn't care to participate in the feud? For now, it seemed to be working.

A big test was awaiting them, though. The night of Emma's pop-up at Eden's had arrived. She was about to burst. Not out of excitement. Out of the worst-ever case of nerves.

Daniel squeezed her hand in the back of the car on the way to Eden's. "You're trembling. Is everything okay?"

She nodded. He did have a way of calming her. "I'll be fine once I get going. I'm just nervous about talking to customers and sounding knowledgeable and like I know what I'm doing. My sisters have put all of this ridiculous pressure on me because of the Princess Emma stuff in the papers, which I guess is my fault. They're sure we'll have a huge turnout tonight. I just want it to go well."

Emma looked down at Daniel's hand wrapped around hers. How she loved his hands. He might spend his days pounding away at his laptop, but there was something so deeply masculine about them. There was nothing better than having his hand at her back, especially when she felt unsure of herself.

"Are you sure you aren't nervous about me being there? About me finally meeting your sisters?"

She didn't want to feel anything less than excited by the prospect of Daniel meeting Mindy and Sophie. Tonight was supposed to be a step forward, for both her relationship with Daniel and the future of the family feud she hoped they could eventually end. But she never really knew how Mindy and Sophie would react to any given situation. They could be cordial, but aloof. She certainly couldn't see them being overly welcoming, even though Emma had told them ahead of time that Daniel was coming.

"I'm excited for them to meet you. I think they'll see things differently after they do. And at least they'll get to see what all the hubbub is about."

"Hubbub?"

A flash of embarrassed warmth hit her cheeks. "Well, you know. Sisters talk. Especially about men." She'd only had a taste of those sisterly moments with Mindy and Sophie, but she'd greatly enjoyed every one.

He nodded. "I see. I only had a brother. And there was far more punching than talking."

Emma disliked that tone in his voice when he talked about William. She could feel his pain when it bubbled to the surface. "You never confided in each other?"

"We did at times. Say if one of us was in a battle of wills with our mother. But most of the time, it was nothing but strong-willed, head-butting sibling rivalry."

"Do you think that had anything to do with him pursuing your fiancée?" Emma still couldn't imagine the betrayal he must have felt at that.

Daniel was quiet and looked out the window.

"You don't have to answer that if you don't want to," she added, feeling desperate. Why she'd decided to dive into this topic, she didn't know, other than she only wanted more of him. She wanted to know everything. "I'm just trying to understand what happened. A betrayal like that is hard to comprehend."

He turned back to her. "It's good for me to talk about it. I don't think I can boil it down to one thing. I'm sure that part of it was jealousy over me getting engaged first. Our mother certainly expected him to be married first. She was merciless about it at the Christmas before the accident. She said he was behind and he'd better catch up. But that's how she got us to be better at everything. She'd pit us against each other."

Emma shook her head. "I'll never understand why anyone would torment someone with such an arbitrary idea, especially a loved one. Her own son, no less. My mother's head is full of rules that have no basis in anything other than the way she sees the world. That's why I never dated. She had me so convinced that all men were terrible and it wasn't worth risking your heart for one."

"Certainly that had to do with your father."

"I'm sure. I mean, she'd gone and fallen in love with her sister's husband." The rest of the story sat perched on Emma's lips. She and Daniel had grown so close and she wanted to keep going. But that meant he had to know that part of what he believed to be true was in fact a lie. "I need to tell you something."

"Anything. Anything at all."

His voice was so measured and calm, she knew she could tell him. "You should know that I didn't grow up in France. Mom and I lived in a small house in New Jersey. She was paid by my father to stay quiet.

And so she did. For my entire life until the day my grandmother's will was read."

"She never told you?"

Emma shook her head. "She told me my father was a deadbeat and that he'd walked away from her before I was born. It's not entirely a lie, but it's also not the truth. He was living right here in Manhattan. I could have had a relationship with him."

"Where did the story about France come from?"

"Sophie and Mindy made it up. It was already bad enough that people found out our father had cheated. So they made up that story to make it seem like the family had known about me all along, and that I'd been taken care of. They were worried the truth would hurt the store and the Eden name."

"I'm so sorry. That's dreadful."

"I went along with it because it made me feel less like a fish out of water. People were quick to accept me. I should have told you earlier, but there was never a good time. And things have moved so fast between us. I didn't want to ruin it. I hope I haven't ruined it now."

Daniel put his finger under her chin and raised it so he could look right at her. His eyes were so caring and warm. "You couldn't ruin it if you tried. It's funny, but we're so alike. We both love our families deeply, but we've suffered because of it."

Emma was so wrapped up in the combination of his face and his words that it was hard to think straight. She loved the moments when they were on the same wavelength. They made her feel nothing less than incredibly lucky that she'd met Daniel at all, let alone had the chance to be with him. "You're so right."

The car pulled up in front of Eden's. A small cluster of photographers was waiting for them outside. She turned to Daniel just as her driver was about to open the door. "You sure you want to do this? We can drive around to another side of the store and bypass this altogether." They'd discussed this back at her apartment and he was adamant that they should make one more exception on the night of her pop-up.

"This is where they're expecting you. You're the star tonight. This isn't about me."

"I still want to know that you're comfortable with it. I know this is difficult."

"As long as you're on my arm, I'm bulletproof."

Emma felt a verifiable squeeze right in the center of her chest. She leaned closer and kissed him on the lips. When she pulled back, she found words circling in her head. Three little words to be exact—*I love you*. But it was too early for that, wasn't it?

Or was it?

She didn't have time to think, let alone say it. Gregory opened the door, and the sounds of the city, traffic and car horns, along with the shouts of the photographers, rushed in.

Emma! Emma!
Over here!
Daniel!

She'd never get used to the idea that the press cared about her, although they clearly did, or at least they liked her with Daniel. Perhaps it was just a sign that people loved controversy, but Emma wanted to put an end to that. There wasn't anything salacious about what she and Daniel were doing—hot, yes, but not wrong. So they'd decided to thumb their noses at some decades-old history. What was the big deal?

She and Daniel came to a stop in the middle of the sidewalk and obligingly posed for a few photographs. He looked as handsome as ever, in a charcoal-gray suit with white shirt and no tie. She loved the little peek of his chest. It left her eager for what might come after the event, when they could go back to their building and be alone. She'd worn a fun navy-blue cocktail dress with a full, knee-length skirt and a low neckline, which Daniel said he liked best on her. In a nod to Sophie, she'd gone with crimson-red Blahniks. It felt like an adventuresome choice.

Emma squeezed Daniel's hand in a steady pattern as the flashbulbs went off. She wanted to remind him that she was thankful for his willingness to endure the public eye. This was hard for him. She knew that. She leaned in and pressed a kiss to his cheek. The flashes went off twice as fast, and she sensed how easily this could turn into a feeding frenzy. Daniel tugged on her arm, and into the revolving door they went, out of one pressure cooker and into the safety of Eden's.

Waiters were on hand with champagne. "Hello, Ms. Stewart," one of them said. "Mr. Stone." They'd clearly been briefed by staff on who would be attending.

"Hi, guys," Emma said. She'd never get used to

deferential treatment, however much it made her feel special.

"Where to?" Daniel asked.

"Straight up to the second floor."

They stepped onto the escalator together and began their ascent. As they rode higher, Daniel's shoulders tightened. Was he that uncomfortable to be at Eden's?

"Is this your first time in the store?"

"Actually, it's my third or fourth time since I've been in New York."

"Oh, really? Spying on us?"

Daniel shook his head and they stepped off the escalator onto the floor that carried the various lines of women's casual wear. The entire department had been condensed into half the normal space, and the open area sectioned off with swaths of sheer silvery fabric hanging from the ceiling, like a glamorous circus tent. Reginald, Eden's creative director, was busy putting the final touches on the displays with his team. Shoppers would be arriving any moment.

"I was merely checking out the competition," Daniel said. "Can you blame me?"

"And? What do you think?"

"It's great."

"The whole thing?" She knew there were parts of the store that fell short. She, Mindy and Sophie were working on it. "You can be honest with me. You won't hurt my feelings."

"Your menswear department is lacking. It needs to be brought into this decade at the very least."

From out of the corner of her eye, Emma spotted

Mindy and Sophie walking toward the pop-up shop from the back of the store, where the bank of executive elevators was. "I want to hear more about that at some point. If you're willing to share."

"I'm more than happy to tell you where you're missing the mark. As for ways to improve what you have, I might need some convincing." He smiled slyly, telling her he was only playing with her.

She leaned in and kissed him. "Something tells me I can find a meaningful form of persuasion."

"I can't wait for that."

"For now, I need you to meet my sisters. I hope you're ready." *I hope I'm ready.*

Again, he took her hand, and that was enough to ward off her trepidation. Mindy and Sophie walked toward them in unison, Mindy showing off her enviable legs in a short emerald-green dress, and Sophie showing hers in a sexy black above-the-knee sheath. They both smiled, their teeth gleaming white, their long red tresses bouncing past their shoulders. They were an intimidating sight, nothing but brute beauty and confidence, but Emma found herself clinging to optimism. Maybe this would all be okay. Maybe today, Sophie and Mindy would welcome with open arms the man Emma cared about so much.

"Finally, we meet Daniel Stone." Mindy was the first to greet him with a handshake, her voice only lightly tinged with skepticism. "I'm Mindy. This is my other sister, Sophie."

Despite Mindy's wary edge, Emma was pleased that she had introduced Sophie as her *other* sister.

Maybe she was finally starting to see Emma as a true part of the family.

"Daniel," Sophie said. "It's nice to meet you. Welcome to Eden's. I hope you have good intentions in visiting the store. And in dating Emma."

Emma nearly choked. This was not Sophie's usual disposition. Not even close.

"Sophie, be nice," Mindy muttered, casting a look over her shoulder. Invited members of the press were filing in.

"I'm sorry, but these are legitimate concerns, and Gram taught me to take any threat to the survival of the store quite seriously." Sophie was now artfully mumbling out of the side of her mouth, as a few reporters strolled past and seemed quite interested in the scene unfolding. "Knowing who his mother is, I'm guessing Daniel has been put on the spot far worse than that."

"Oh, I have," he said.

A reporter waved at Sophie and she politely returned the gesture. Then she sucked in a deep breath, forced a smile and looked Daniel square in the face. "More than anything, I need to know that you're going to be kind to Emma. Because if you aren't, if you're playing at some other game, Mr. Stone, there will be problems."

"That's really what this is about," Mindy said, patting Daniel on the shoulder. "If you hurt her, you'll have three angry women on your hands, not just one. Trust me, no man wants to go up against the Eden sisters."

Emma swallowed hard. She wasn't sure she'd breathed once during that exchange. It was a tad horrifying to watch her sisters launch thinly veiled threats at Daniel. They were behaving like glamorous mobsters. But after having felt left out so many times, it felt good to know they had her back. It didn't matter to them that Daniel was handsome and wealthy and powerful. They would take on a man who didn't treat her well.

The crowd had grown significantly as the first wave of shoppers and members of the media arrived.

Mindy patted Daniel on the shoulder again. "You don't have anything to worry about. If you're a decent guy, everything will be fine."

Daniel turned, looking down at Emma. "Then I truly don't have a thing to worry about. I'm more than a decent guy."

"That's the spirit," Mindy said. "Now if you'll excuse me, I have a boyfriend to track down and shoppers to schmooze with."

"Yes. We should be spending time with our customers," Sophie said. A large gathering of their guests had assembled inside the pop-up. "It's your night, Emma. You lead the way."

And to think Emma had worried about chatting with shoppers. That was going to be a piece of cake compared to what they'd just experienced with Sophie and Mindy. "Time to get to work." She tugged on Daniel's hand. "You coming?"

"For you? Of course."

* * *

Daniel downed another glass of champagne to take the edge off. He wasn't surprised that Sophie and Mindy had questioned his intentions. It was more a shock that they'd done it so fiercely. Still, he would've been lying if he'd said he didn't enjoy watching Emma, Mindy and Sophie in action. He kept to the periphery of the pop-up, observing the interactions of the shoppers and the three sisters. They mingled with customers, they chatted and encouraged purchases. One thing was certain—everyone seemed to be thoroughly enjoying themselves. They couldn't snatch up items fast enough. This had been a brilliant idea on Sophie Eden's part. One he might have to steal and adapt for Stone's.

Of course, Emma was the main source of his attention, but he did enjoy observing the dynamic between the sisters. Despite the confrontational approach she'd taken in meeting him, Sophie was the peacemaker, a bridge between Emma and Mindy. Mindy was the watchful eye, the hawk who made sure everyone was okay.

Emma brought unbridled enthusiasm to the table, especially when speaking with their customers. She certainly didn't act like a woman with billions in the bank. She was warm and gracious, and they were all suitably charmed. Born a Brit and having lived in England his entire life, Daniel was well aware of the allure of royalty. You got swept up in it, even when you knew deep down that notions of one family being more important than another were nonsense. He despised the press, but they'd been so right about one thing—Emma came off exactly like a princess, graceful and warm and utterly breathtaking. He only hoped the tabloids didn't decide to tear her off her pedestal. In his experience, they loved to love you, until they decided that ripping you to pieces would sell papers.

Daniel's phone buzzed in his pocket. Emma was preoccupied with a woman and her male companion, so he distanced himself from the crowd as well as he could, though there were people everywhere at this point. He wound his way past the other guests, down one of the wide white marble-floored aisles between departments. He didn't want to be that person—the one with his nose in his phone while standing in the midst of a crowd.

He had a text from Charlotte Locke.

Lease terms accepted. Sign papers Monday 2:00?

Daniel read the message twice. This was good news. To the Daniel of a few weeks ago, the one who'd never laid eyes on Emma Stewart, this was a fantastic development. Everything he'd worked for, everything his mother wanted. The space was perfect. It was time to make his move.

But he found his thumb hovering over the keyboard, unable to type a reply to Charlotte. Why was he hesitating? What was holding him back? He heard Emma's exuberant laugh over the din of the crowd and turned to see her smiling and tossing back her hair. No matter what they'd agreed to, it still seemed unlikely that this wouldn't come between them. Eden's was her whole life, a tether to the one thing she'd said she'd always wanted to be a part of—a family.

If he did things right, the existence of Stone's New York would threaten that. And if he failed, the amount of his family's money down the drain would be devastating. It would give his mother more than enough reason to put off her retirement another five or ten years. Daniel didn't think he could live through that. He couldn't deal with her constantly breathing down his neck. It was too much part and parcel of living in the shadow of William.

He and Emma were going to have to talk about this, in depth, before he could sign the lease. He wasn't going to pull the rug out from under her that way. It had nothing to do with Mindy's and Sophie's threats and everything to do with wanting to treat Emma with the respect and courtesy she deserved. He had to let her know that he was about to do something that would turn up the heat. He just had to find the right time, and fast. Perhaps a getaway was in order. Something romantic, if only for a few nights. Today was Thursday. They could leave Saturday and return Monday morning in time for him to do what his job and his family required.

He tapped out his response. Great news. I'll be there Monday. Thx.

He further distanced himself from the crowd and sent his mother a text. Lease is a go. Signing Monday. More soon. That should be enough to keep her happy. At least for a little while.

He stuffed his phone back into his pocket as a towering man wearing an all-black ensemble of suit, shirt and tie approached.

The man held out his hand. "You must be Daniel Stone. Sam Blackwell."

Daniel was stuck for a moment. According to Emma, Sam had played a role in convincing Charlotte Locke to drop him. "Ah, yes. Mr. Blackwell."

"Please. Call me Sam. Our girlfriends are sisters."

"That's not our only connection now, is it?"

Sam's dark eyes lit up. "I know. I'm sorry about that. All's fair in love and war, right?"

"It's not really my style, but we all have our methods." Daniel's upbringing demanded at least a veneer of politeness, but he could see why Sam rubbed so many people the wrong way.

"I can tell you the sisters feel that way. These three take their business very seriously. Does make me wonder what exactly your end game is. The business rivalry has to be a bone of contention. Or are you just getting your fun while you can?"

Daniel bristled at the suggestion, even when he understood exactly why Sam was asking the question. "Emma and I enjoy each other's company greatly. That's all we care to focus on."

"I think Mindy's still figuring her out. They've definitely butted heads a few times."

Daniel felt a deep need to defend Emma, even when he knew she was strong and didn't need rescuing. What was there to figure out about Emma? She was open and loyal, resilient and big-hearted.

"Emma's had a difficult life. She wants to claim her role at Eden's and in that family. It hasn't been easy for her to find a place between two sisters who've known each other their entire lives. She's been forced to play a lot of catch-up."

"Emma has been more than compensated for any hardships. She's a billionaire. She'll never worry about money ever again. She grew up in a French chateau with lavender fields and a private chef. It's not like she's suffered."

"That's not entirely accurate." Daniel was surprised at the force with which those words left his mouth, but it was worse than inaccurate. It was an outright lie.

"Oh, really? Are you saying I don't know the whole story?"

Daniel wasn't about to share a single detail with Sam. He had no way of knowing if Mindy chose to share the same things with Sam that Emma had shared with him. "Perhaps you should ask Mindy about that." Daniel shouldn't have let himself get angry, but his protective side had taken over. He was beginning to despise the way Emma's family had treated her.

"That's all you're going to say?"

Daniel cleared his throat. He saw no reason to answer. "You'll have to excuse me. I'm going to check on Emma and see if she needs anything."

"Yeah. Not a bad idea. I should see if Mindy will let us get out of here any time soon."

Daniel took long strides to get to Emma. She

glanced over at him as he approached and their gazes connected, her brown eyes as inviting as ever. Would there ever come a time when he wouldn't feel that zap of electricity between them? Emma grinned, then returned her attention to the customer she'd been speaking with. "Thank you so much for coming this evening. I hope your daughter enjoys the perfume."

The woman left and Daniel took his chance, smoothing his hand across Emma's back and tugging her against his side. "How much longer?"

Emma surveyed the remaining customers. "An hour? Maybe less if people make their purchases." She looked up into Daniel's eyes. "Why? Are you bored?"

"No. I'm just eager to get you home."

An effortless smile crossed her sumptuous lips. "Home? Does that mean my place or yours?"

"Whichever place makes you most comfortable."

"What did you have in mind? TV? A walk with the dogs?" She ran her slender fingers along the edge of his jacket lapel.

How he loved it when she was being playful. Everything felt more exciting. He leaned down and settled his mouth on her ear, inhaling her sweet perfume. "I want to get you out of that dress. I want to leave you gasping my name."

"I could use some unwinding."

He kissed the side of her neck. "Don't worry. I'm on it."

Daniel stayed by Emma's side as she chatted with the remaining big-roller customers, every minute an exercise in patience. He wanted her so badly right now it felt as if the seconds were ticking by impossibly slowly. Every subtle brush of their skin, every knowing glance was torture.

He tried to stem the tide by staying in the moment, but that only brought to mind what his family would say if they could see him, spending time on enemy territory and feeling, quite honestly, like an invading army. Ever since the night of the opera, he'd thought once or twice that perhaps his parents would change their minds about the Edens once they'd met Emma. But after meeting Mindy and Sophie, he knew it was going to take a lot. They were just as entrenched and invested in the hatred as his side. What a waste.

"I need to check something in my office," Emma said, when it was finally time to go. Eden's employees were cleaning up and restocking the pop-up, which would remain open the next day for the general public. Mindy and Sam had long since left. Sophie was making her way to the escalator with her fiancé, Jake.

Daniel hoped her sisters had taken the time to tell her she'd done a good job or congratulated her for what had clearly been a successful evening. "Tonight was incredible. Well done," he said, when they reached Emma's office upstairs.

She walked behind her desk and hit a key on her computer keyboard. "Do you think it went well?"

"Are you kidding? It was unbelievable. It's a fabulous concept, but I think you did a particularly bang-up job. Your sisters should be more appreciative."

"So you noticed. They didn't say a thing to me."

"I wondered about that. I don't like it. Not one bit."

She shrugged her lovely shoulders and scanned her computer screen. She shook her head.

"Everything okay?" he asked.

"Yeah. I was just looking for an email. I get them on my phone, but sometimes my work messages don't always make it through."

"Hopefully, it'll be there tomorrow morning." He didn't want either of them to have to think about work anymore. They'd both had enough of that for tonight.

"It better be. I've been waiting for it for a while."

Emma was holding something back from him. He could hear it in her voice. These were the moments when Daniel most sensed the ways the businesses could come between them. "I meant what I said. You did a fantastic job and your sisters should tell you so."

"They work hard, too. We're all working our butts off. I'm sure I need to be better about telling them the same things." She waved it off. "It's fine. I don't need constant reassurance. I'm confident that I did a good job tonight."

Once again, Daniel felt a need to protect Emma from the forces around her—the store, which had her hemmed into obligations, and her sisters, who weren't appreciative enough. He knew exactly what it was like to be in that situation. "You did better than good. You were a star. It's no accident that you've garnered so much media attention. The press can't take their eyes off you." He found his pulse pounding in his ears. This was what she did to him when they were alone. "*I* can't take my eyes off you." *I love you* nearly escaped his lips. He sucked it back in, his head reeling. It had come out of nowhere, a force of nature, like a summer storm that swooped in and leveled everything in its path.

"You are too sweet to me, Daniel Stone. If you aren't careful, the world's going to find out that you're not the cutthroat businessman everyone thinks you are."

"I vote that we keep that secret between you and me."

"As long as you make it worth my while, I can keep my mouth shut."

Another wave of heat rolled over him. They might not make it home. "I like it better when your mouth is open." He claimed her lips with his, giving in to every sexy thought Emma had provoked in him this evening. His hand slid to her hip, his fingers curling into the soft flesh of her bottom as their tongues wound together, hot and wet. Emma leaned back against her desk and he gathered the skirt of her dress, dragging the fabric up until his hand found the silky skin of her inner thigh.

She bowed into him, moaning against his mouth. "Yes, Daniel. I want you." She reared her head back, eyes frantically scanning his face. "The door."

Daniel needed no further instruction, crossing the room in two long strides while he cast aside his jacket. With a click of the lock and a flick of the light switch, they had the privacy he'd been so desperate for all night. "Don't move." He rushed back behind her desk where she was sitting, legs dangling off the edge. "Tell me you'll leave the shoes on."

The large window behind him glowed with light from the city. She grinned. "I'll leave the shoes on."

He unbuttoned his trousers and let them fall to the floor. His pelvis was buzzing with electricity. Just like every other time with Emma, he was so hard so fast that he wondered how there was enough blood to circulate through the rest of his body. He needed her so badly he ached. He unbuttoned his shirt while Emma reached down and took his erection in her hand. Her fingers were cool against his overheated skin.

"Mmm," she hummed, resting her chin on his bare chest and stroking firmly.

"You're going to drive me mad." He could hardly keep his eyes open. Her touch felt so impossibly good.

"Then take off my dress." She scooted forward and hopped off the desk, pulling her hair to one side and presenting her back to him.

"I plan to." He urged her closer to the window, dragging down the zipper.

"Daniel. Somebody will see."

He slipped her dress from her shoulders and pushed it to the floor. Emma covered her breasts with her hands, looking back at him, questioning.

"Don't you trust me?" he asked. "No one can see us up here. We're all alone."

She nodded. "I do trust you. Implicitly."

"Good." He pressed the full length of his body against hers, his chest to her back. He gathered her hair and kissed her neck, her shoulder, then down the channel of her spine as he tugged her silky panties from her legs.

Emma stepped out of them, now wearing only those sexy heels, leaving her beautiful naked form before him. She turned and he gripped her rib cage with both hands, his thumbs pushing up on her full breasts. He lowered his head and sucked her nipple into his mouth, swirling his tongue. He loved the way she reacted to him, the way the pink bud gathered and tightened. He loved how sweet she tasted. He couldn't get enough of the soft moans that escaped her lips. All he could think about was being inside her. All he wanted was to make her writhe with pleasure.

He let go of her nipple, giving it a few quick flicks with his tongue before turning her toward the window. He could see their reflections in the glass, could see the anticipation on her face, her mouth slightly slack and her eyes dark with desire. She liked that this felt a little dangerous, and that made him even more turned on. He reached down for his trousers and pulled a condom from his pocket. He'd brought one in case they ended up at her apartment. He hadn't taken the time to consider they might not make it home. He rolled it on and positioned himself behind her, urging her to bend forward, and pulling her hips closer. Emma reached out and placed one hand against the window, gasping as he slipped his fingers between her legs to make sure she was ready for him.

"You're so wet," he muttered.

"That's because I want you."

He drove inside her, his eyes clamping shut as he

gave up all rational thought and sank into the magnificent warmth of her body. He reached around with both hands and caressed her breasts, teasing her nipples with his fingertips. The noises that left her lips told him he was doing everything right, but he knew he could do better, so he slid one hand down her belly and found her apex, spreading her folds with his fingers and rubbing in determined circles.

"That feels so good," she muttered, moving against him.

He opened his eyes, unable to decide what to look at first—the creamy skin of her bottom as he drove his hips into her, or the reflection of her full breast in his hand, her mouth gaping and her eyes closed. Once again she was a feast for the senses. Everything he ever wanted in the most tempting package.

The tension was wrapping tight around his hips, the muscles of his groin aching for release. Emma's breaths were shorter now, the moans deeper and almost continuous. Her muscles were starting to tighten around his length, pulsing stronger with every thrust. He knew she was close. He only hoped he could hang on until she came. He was right at his peak, carnal forces threatening to push him over the edge, when Emma called out, "Daniel."

He grinned for an instant before the orgasm slammed into him, enveloping his body in so much warmth and bliss he could hardly support his own weight. Emma pulsed around him, prolonging the pleasure. This had been so worth waiting for. Emma straightened and turned, pressing her chest against his and kissing him hard.

"That was a surprise," she panted.

He smiled with the best sense of pride imaginable. "I want to keep you on your toes."

"Or in heels." She kissed him again, her lips soft and tender against his. "You're unbelievable. You put up with my sisters and my work event and then you seduce me in my office. I'm trying to think of a time a guy has ever been so generous with me, and I know for a fact that it's never happened."

Again, he was proud of these feelings he was able to build in her. Probably because he knew very well by now that this was a two-way street. She was uncovering so many things in him that he'd long thought were gone—hope and happiness and, quite possibly, love.

"Let's go away," he blurted.

"What? Where?" Her face was full of surprise.

"Bermuda. I have a beautiful house there, right on the beach. It's quiet and warm, and most importantly, we can be alone. It's only a two and a half hour flight from New York. I'll charter a plane."

"Really?" There was that sound he adored— Emma's bubbly excitement.

"Yes, really. I know that neither of us can get away for long. Two nights? This weekend?"

"I suppose Mindy and Sophie would be okay with that."

"You work hard, I work hard, and I want us to be able to spend some time together away from things like the press and your sisters. It'll be just the two of us. We can swim and take naps and make love all afternoon." Simply saying the words ushered in the most beautiful fantasy he could imagine. He might not ever want to come back.

"You sure you'll be able to pull the trip together so quickly?"

He had to show up on Monday afternoon to sign the lease. He had to have the chance to break the news to her before he made that one crucial move. "If you can make it work, I will make it happen."

She drew a finger down the center of his chest. "I'll make it work."

Ten

The morning after Emma's pop-up, Mindy opened the door of her apartment to pick up her daily copy of the newspaper. It didn't stay in her hands for long. She read the headline and it promptly slipped from her fingers and fell to the floor. "Oh no." The ugly words practically screamed at her from the front page.

Eden Family Hid Heiress: Princess Emma a dirty secret.

Her heart started pounding, her mind racing. The press had found out. They knew what Mindy and Sophie had wanted so badly to keep hidden, Sophie especially. This was enough to take down more than the store. It could destroy the entire Eden family. The affair that produced Emma would be all anyone would ever remember about their father. The fact that he and Gram had paid Emma's mother hush money for years? That would be their shared legacy. Not Eden's department store. The story would always be tainted by sex and money, the only things anyone seemed interested in these days, anyway.

Mindy bent down and picked up the paper, closing her front door and forcing herself to read. She knew every bit of the tale, and most of what the story said was true, although there was certainly conjecture. She didn't know for sure that Emma had ever lived in a mouse-infested house. Mindy supposed she should have asked. She should have spent some time getting to know Emma a bit better. For the moment, she had to figure out where the press had gotten this story in the first place. How had anyone known to dig? Emma was supposed to be the media's princess. Now she'd been reduced to a dirty secret.

Mindy marched into the kitchen and quickly made coffee. Today was going to require a lot of caffeine. This story could very well mean that her own business could be ruined. Gone in the blink of an eye. In the age of tabloid firing squads and internet witch hunts, she knew exactly how damaging a story like this could be.

Coffee made, she rushed back to her room, two mugs in hand. Sam was sound asleep in her bed. She set down his cup and, holding the other, sat on the edge of the mattress. She hoped her movements might wake him, but Sam slept like the dead. Maybe it was the sex. He did have a real talent for wearing her out. And he always wanted it. Always.

She drew in a deep breath and studied him. With his eyes closed in peaceful slumber, he was remarkably nice to look at. Long and muscled, with touchable, jet-black hair that held a slight wave. He was her beautiful problem. She wanted him more than almost anything, but time and again, he'd proved how adept he was at disrupting everything. If he wanted to make trouble, he did. With aplomb. Something about that newspaper article was telling her that he'd done it again.

"Sam. Wake up."

He rolled to his back and his bracing blue eyes popped open. This was already a good sign. He was usually impossible to rouse without the promise of sex. "Let me guess. There's a story in the newspaper."

She smacked his arm. "So you are behind this." She tossed the publication across the bed and it landed in the center of his chest.

He lifted his head and ruffled the pages, squinting to read. "Oh, wow. That's quite a headline, isn't it?"

"It's horrible. How am I going to explain to Sophie and Emma that you were behind this?" Mindy didn't fear her sisters' ire so much, as she'd been trying to convince them that Sam wasn't a bad guy. This would do more than set back her efforts. It might be the final nail in the coffin. It might be confirmation that she needed to cut Sam loose. For real this time. No second chances. Or third or fourth.

"So don't explain it. It's not your job to prevent this from happening. Sophie and Emma bear just as much of the brunt of this secret as you do. Just tell them there must be a leak in the store."

"There isn't a leak. Sophie will never believe that. She trusts everyone implicitly. Besides, no one knows about this. Just me, Sophie and Emma."

"That's not entirely true. You told me some of it and I heard the rest from Daniel Stone."

A strange mix of shock and vindication rushed through Mindy's veins. She and Sophie had been so sure that Emma's involvement with Daniel would backfire on them all. Sure, Sam had fired the shots, but it appeared that Daniel had given him ammunition. "I can't believe she told him. She was under strict orders to keep her mouth shut."

"Orders? Is Emma not an equal partner? It seems to me like you and Sophie spend an awful lot of time telling her what to do." Sam rolled to his side and propped his head up with his hand. His splendid naked chest was on full display, the sheet dipping temptingly low, beneath the trail of hair under his belly button. For a moment, Mindy forgot what they were talking about.

"She doesn't always know what she's doing. She's new to this whole world. She knows nothing about running a business. If we don't guide her, it'll be a disaster."

"I'm not sure that's true, either. She seems to have a natural affinity for enticing the press. That's not an easy thing to accomplish."

Mindy crossed her arms. "Will you stop reminding me how amazing Princess Emma is? Whose side are you on, anyway?"

A cocky smile crossed his lips. "I knew you were jealous. That's why I leaked the story. I thought it would make you happy to have her knocked down a few pegs. I can guarantee there will be no more princess stories. It'll all be about poor, sad Emma."

Was Mindy jealous? Was that her problem? Was that why she'd been so hesitant to trust Emma and her choices? "She's still my sister. I don't want her dragged through the mud. Nor do I want my entire family and our name becoming a disgrace."

"You sure you feel that way about her?"

Mindy couldn't have said that for certain in January, when Emma was new at the store and new to the family, back when Mindy and Sophie were still reeling from learning they had to share the four-billion-dollar inheritance three ways rather than two. But seeing her on the cover of the paper this morning, all Mindy could think was how this was going to shake Emma's confidence, just when she should be on top of the world. It wasn't fair. Mindy knew what it was like to be on top and have things go upside down. That's what had happened to her when she'd been forced by their grandmother's will to work for Eden's and set aside her own company.

"Part of me wants to protect her. Of course. Sophie and I both feel that way. We're still getting to know her, though. It's a ridiculous situation."

"One you can thank your father and grandmother for."

Mindy pressed her lips together tightly. "I know. They messed up. Big time." Any realizations she was coming to right now about Emma were quickly being overshadowed by the larger looming problem. Sam needed to go. She was sleeping with a man who made a lot of assumptions and was in no way scared to act on impulse. He kept thinking he would make her happy, and all he did was make her situation worse.

"Sam. I don't think we can be together anymore. I don't think it's going to work. Sophie doesn't like you. Emma might never speak to you after she finds out what you did. And I can't help it. My family is important to me. They might drive me crazy sometimes, but I can't alienate them for a guy."

"Is that what I am to you? Just some guy?" Sam tore back the sheet and climbed out of bed. "I put multiple business trips on hold so I could be with you. I went to that silly event at the store, and listened to you come home every night and complain about your sisters. Do you not understand that I don't do that for just anyone?"

"I'm supposed to be impressed that you'd be willing to hang around for two weeks?" Mindy could never have a future with Sam if he was going to treat her like an inconvenience. The things she'd asked of him were perfectly reasonable. She wouldn't be told any different. She stood and tightened the tie on her robe. "You need to go."

"You tell me to go and I'm not coming back. Ever."

Mindy absorbed every word he said, knowing exactly how determined he would be to keep his promise. There would be no going back. She bit on her lower lip before mustering the strength to push him all the way out of her life. "I know. My sisters need me more than I need you." Even she was surprised by how harsh her words were.

"Have it your way, Min. Good luck with your dysfunctional family."

She walked out of the room, waiting until she got into the hall to let the tears stream down her face. Mindy didn't cry often, but this hurt. Sam Blackwell had an inexplicable hold on her heart. He was going to be impossible to forget.

Daniel woke to the sound of Emma's cell phone ringing in the other room.

"Emma. Darling." Half-awake, he pressed a kiss to her bare shoulder. "Your phone's ringing. Shall I get it for you?"

She pried one eye open. "What time is it?"

"A bit after seven."

"It has to be Mindy. She's the only one who calls me this early." The ringing stopped. "Oh, good. She gave up." Emma scooted closer to Daniel and nudged his chest with her nose. "I'm not ready to get out of this bed."

From the foot of the bed, Jolly yipped. "Someone's not happy we're snuggling without her." Daniel was about to evict Jolly from the room when Emma's phone rang again.

"Ugh." She threw back the covers and grabbed a

T-shirt of Daniel's, which was slung over the back of a chair. "I'd better see what she wants."

Daniel took this as his cue that their day had begun. He climbed out of bed and dressed in another of his T-shirts and a pair of track pants. The instant he stepped out into the hall, he heard the distress in Emma's voice.

"Oh my God. Are you serious?"

Daniel rushed to her side, placing his hand at the small of her back. When Emma turned to him, her forehead was wrinkled with worry, her eyes tormented.

"What's wrong?" he whispered.

"Okay. I'll be in as soon as I can," she said into the phone. "We'll meet at nine?" She nodded. "Yes. Bye." Emma pressed the end button and pinched the bridge of her nose with two fingers, her eyes clamped shut.

"What's going on?" he asked.

"There's a story in the paper this morning."

"About last night?"

She shook her head. All color had drained from her face. "About me. My past. Everything my father and grandmother did to hide me from the world. The lies. The money. Everything."

Daniel's stomach lurched. If he was responsible for this, he'd never forgive himself. "Do they know who fed this information to the press?"

"That was actually Sophie calling, not Mindy. She said Mindy confessed it was Sam. He's had it in his head for months that if he messes things up for the store, it'll get Mindy out from under the obligation."

Daniel had to come clean. He couldn't drop this bomb on her in Bermuda. He already had a big enough one waiting. He hated having any at all. "I talked to Sam last night. I slipped about New Jersey. I don't think he knew."

Emma's eyes became as large as saucers. "No. Daniel. Mindy and Sophie can't know that I told you anything. I never should have said anything. I was supposed to keep it a secret."

"He was trying to say that it didn't matter that you've had a hard life, because you inherited so much money. I had to defend you. I'm so sorry."

Emma walked away from him, pacing the living room, bare feet padding across the hardwood floors. "Sophie has been saying for months that she doesn't trust Sam. I can't believe Mindy said anything. She's always harping on me to keep my mouth closed." She pressed the home button on her phone and the screen came to life. "I have to see what the paper says. It's just going to make me upset, but I need to know."

Daniel reached out for her arm. "Do you want me to read it first?"

"If I'm going to be an embarrassment to the store and my family, I'd like to know exactly what I'm up against." She scanned the screen.

Daniel read over her shoulder. *That headline.* A dirty secret. A sob left Emma's lips and she sank down onto the couch.

"Let me see." He took her phone from her. Despite everything, the first photo brought a smile to his face—of him and Emma in front of Eden's last night. She was radiant as always, but the affection that had grown between them was plain as day. As fake as the tabloids could be, that picture was real. His mother was going to see that picture. She would know he hadn't shared the full scope of his relationship with Emma.

"Well?" she asked.

"It's everything you told me. But you didn't tell me that your mom home-schooled you to keep you away from people. You didn't tell me that she hid the money from you."

Emma buried her head in her hands. "Oh, God. That's in there?"

He put his arm around her shoulders, desperately wanting to comfort her. "This is why I hate the press."

"I want to hate them, but they're telling the truth."

"I'm still sorry this happened. And I'm sorry your mother lied to you all those years. No one should ever be treated like that."

She lifted her head, staring off into space. "I don't blame her. I don't. Of course she didn't trust my dad. He bribed her to keep their child a secret. So that's why she hid the money. She was so worried that he would stop paying and somehow manage to ruin her if she dared to speak out."

No wonder Emma had once had so little trust of men. Her father, the most important man in her life, had acted so horribly toward her and her mother. "I'm so sorry. But you have an amazing life now and a wonderful job and more than enough money to live off." *And there's us.*

Emma looked at him, shaking her head. "My amazing life is never going to be the same. Every time I go to a party or work or even just walk through the lobby of our building, everyone's going to know the smallest details about the worst things that have ever happened to me. They'll know that I don't really come from wealth and power and influence. I'm just a girl who grew up with nothing and stumbled into an inheritance. I hardly know what I'm doing at work most of the time. Sophie and Mindy know it, too."

Daniel pulled her into his arms. He'd never had to worry about the things she had, and he wished he could take her pain away. "If anyone thinks any less of you because of this, they don't deserve to know you or have you in their life. There are plenty of people who don't care about the money or the designer dresses or the fancy parties. You don't have anything to live up to, Emma. You're perfect just the way you are."

"You didn't notice me at all until I was wearing a ten-thousand-dollar designer dress and so much makeup I could hardly hold my head up."

Daniel wasn't making anything better. She wasn't wrong on that point. "And I feel like an ass for it. I know I apologized then, but I'll apologize again. I'm sorry. I came to New York for business and nothing else." Just thinking about his state of mind when he'd arrived made him realize just how much Emma had changed him. He didn't recognize the man he was about to describe. "I was trying to find a way to live up to my brother's memory, and now I'm sitting here

telling you that trying to live up to anyone else's expectations is pointless. I understand that you don't
want to disappoint your family, but you can't forget
that in a lot of ways, your family let you down."

A tear leaked out of her eye, followed by another.
She tried to blink them away, and she looked up at the
ceiling as if she could hold it all in. "I just want to find
a place where I belong. A place where I can be me."

He wrapped her up in his arms, rocking her back
and forth and pressing his lips to the top of her head.
"You can belong with me. I always want you to just
be you."

"No fancy designer gowns?"

He kissed her temple. "I'm fine with whatever you
want to wear. Or not wear. Totally up to you."

She laughed quietly, resting her head on his shoulder. "Thank you. That makes me feel a little better. I
don't know what I would do without you."

"I feel the same way." With those words, Daniel
knew that this trip to Bermuda tomorrow had to be
more than just the sharing of a few uncomfortable
truths. He couldn't let Emma slip away. He loved her.
"I'd say the timing of our trip tomorrow couldn't be
any better."

"Yes. I need a vacation now more than anything."
She sat back and wiped the tears from her eyes.
"Thank you for talking me off the ledge. Thank you
for everything."

"Of course."

"Unfortunately, I need to get into the office so my
sisters and I can have it out."

"You can blame it all on me."

"Something tells me that's not how it went down."

"Everything will be okay. It will all work out. I promise." He knew he had no business making assurances like that, but he would have done anything to make it all okay.

She sighed heavily, her shoulders dropping. "Maybe. Hopefully. What are you going to do today?"

"Work. Run an errand or two."

"Stay out of trouble."

"I will." He smiled, hoping it wasn't considered trouble to go shopping for a ring.

Emma called Duane and let him know ahead of time that she was on her way to Eden's. He got rid of any photographers by having Lizzie feed them a fake tip on her way into the building, stopping and whispering that she'd seen Emma down the block at Starbucks.

Emma was immensely thankful to be able to walk quietly into the store. Her life plan from now on involved zero red carpets, minimal publicity and avoiding attention whenever possible. Princess Emma was dead now. The media had killed her.

Up on the executive floor, Emma stepped off the elevator and Lizzie bolted out of her seat, but Emma already knew what she was going to say.

"I know. I know. They're waiting for me in Sophie's office. Did I get a call from anyone at Nora Bradford's?"

"No. Not this morning."

"Shoot." Emma was tired of stressing about this. Eden's had agreed to Nora's conditions. Why was the paperwork delayed?

"I'll put them right through if they call." Lizzie stepped out from behind her desk. "I'm so sorry about the tabloid story."

"Thank you. Me, too."

"If it helps at all, it doesn't make me think less of you. In fact, it makes me like you more. You could have told everyone from the beginning. It would have been fine."

"It doesn't make you look at Eden's differently? My grandmother? My father?"

Lizzie grimaced. "Yes. I suppose that left a bad taste behind."

Tell me about it. "I'd better go speak with my sisters." Emma hustled into her office, set down her bag and checked her email. Nothing there from Nora Bradford's team. As soon as she was done with Mindy and Sophie, she was going to have to make another call.

She pushed back from her desk and strode into Sophie's office. "I'm here. Whether you like it or not."

She was so over everything right now. All she could think about was getting to Bermuda with Daniel. She so looked forward to forty-eight hours of getting lost in him and shutting out everything else.

"That's a terrible attitude," Mindy said. "But I get it."

"It was Sam. Just so you know," Sophie said by

way of interjection. "He fed the story to one of the reporters at the pop-up last night."

"Nice. Real nice," Mindy said. "You're just a ray of sunshine lately, aren't you?"

"She deserves to know the truth. Your boyfriend is a jerk. He's the reason we're in this predicament."

"He's no longer my boyfriend, so you can stop referring to him that way. I kicked him out of my apartment this morning." Mindy chewed on her thumbnail.

"For good?" Sophie asked.

"It's over. Done. I don't want to talk about it."

Emma and Sophie looked at each other, silently agreeing that this was a good thing. Mindy didn't seem too overly broken up over it. Emma took a seat. "I don't think it's all Sam's fault. Daniel slipped and said something about France not being the whole story."

"So you *both* told your boyfriends the story that we promised to keep a secret between the three of us." Sophie crossed her arms and sat back in her chair, shaking her head. "This makes our whole family look so bad. Both Dad and Gram would be horrified to know that this came out."

Emma dug her nails into the heels of her hands. Looking bad was one thing, living an entire life on the receiving end of a family secret was another. Neither Mindy nor Sophie seemed to grasp that. "I don't know how they would feel about it. I never really knew either of them." This was still very much the elephant in the room whenever their dad or grandmother came up in conversation. Emma had been robbed of those relationships.

"Why are you spending so much time worrying about what Dad and Gram would think?" Mindy shot a look at Sophie, "They're both dead. Why don't you spend some time thinking about how Emma must feel? She's the real victim in this."

Sophie sat frozen. So did Emma. How could anyone have ever known that Mindy would rush to her defense?

"It still reflects badly on the family and on the store. It makes us all look horrible," Sophie said.

"Of course it does. But we can't stuff the genie back in the bottle. We can't undo what's been done. We have to figure out what our next step is. We have to move on." Mindy sucked in a deep breath, as if she was getting ready to unleash even more. Perhaps her breakup with Sam had put her that much more on edge. "Emma, you should know that neither Sophie nor I was close to our father. Whatever you're thinking you lost out on with him, it didn't exist. He wasn't around for us, and when he was, we were nothing but a disappointment to him. Especially me."

"Mindy…" Sophie started.

"No. Soph. It's true. Dad thought girls should only be sweet and quiet, and I was neither of those things. I was serious. I was focused on school and career. He hated every guy I ever dated. He was always needling me to look for good husband material. Whatever that's supposed to mean. Clearly, I haven't learned much." Mindy shook her head and closed her eyes for a moment. For the first time, Emma saw real pain on her face.

"He definitely had dysfunctional attitudes about women," Sophie said. "Gram always fought him on it, but I think it was his way of rebelling against a mother who was just larger than life."

"He showed our mom zero respect." Mindy said, turning to Emma. "He showed your mother no respect. He simply wasn't a nice person. So you didn't miss out on anything where he's concerned. I promise you that. I loved him, but only because he's my dad. It has nothing to do with any true affection for the man."

"I… I had no idea," Emma said, unsure if this made her feel better or simply made her sad. It certainly made her heart go out to both Sophie and Mindy.

"If you think about it, Gram gave him his just deserts when she wrote you into the will, Emma," Mindy continued. "She'd made a promise to keep his secret, but she also made sure that at least part of it came out when she died. But the three of us never promised to be the steward of those lies. And we made a mistake when we tried to do that. It's even worse that we made up something else."

"I felt like it was the best thing for the store," Sophie said. "We were already struggling, and the second Gram died, all signs were pointing to the store going right along with her."

"I know, and I backed you up at the time, but it was a mistake. We covered up Emma's history, and she's our sister. We can't treat each other like this. We have to be a unified front or we're going to fail. If we care at all about honoring Gram's legacy, we need to own up to everything that came out and focus on the store. If we can't be real with people, I have to wonder what we're doing."

Emma wasn't sure she'd taken a breath at all in the last several minutes. Not only because she'd just been handed a lot of information to unpack, but because she'd had no idea Mindy felt this way about any of it.

"I thought you hated the store," Sophie said to Mindy.

"I don't hate it. I love the store. I just don't love the timing. If this had happened five years from now, I might have been more settled with my own business. But that's not how things happened. And the reality of it is that if it had gone on for five more years, that would have meant all that time Emma would have been living without what was rightly hers."

"I hadn't thought about that," Sophie said.

"The thing I figured out this morning, as I was looking at the man I stupidly fell for, is that you two are the only people in the world I can really trust," Mindy said. "That's the way it should be. We're sisters. There is no stronger bond than that. And we have to stick together. No more secrets. We keep everything out in the open."

"How does this strike you, Emma?" Sophie asked. "It's your story that's all over the papers today. You have to decide which version of your history you want out there. Even if it damages the Eden name, you're still the one who has to live with it."

Several weeks ago, Emma might have been tempted to go on clinging to the lie. It made life easier. But it wasn't right. She was who she was, and as bizarre a journey as her life had been thus far, as much as it had caused her pain, she wouldn't have traded it for anything. "Keeping secrets is too much work. I don't see any point in hiding any of it anymore."

It was quiet in Sophie's office for a good minute or more, all three of them nodding and thinking. "Okay, then," Sophie said. "That's settled. If anyone asks, we say it's all true."

"Did you really live in a house infested with mice?" Mindy asked. "I'm so sorry if that's the case."

"We did have a few mice for a few weeks one winter. It wasn't a big deal. The neighbor brought her cat over and that was the end of that." Emma disliked that look of pity on her sisters' faces, but she was going to have to live with that. She'd likely get that treatment a lot in the coming weeks as people got used to the real version of her past.

"So what's the story with Daniel?" Sophie asked. "I mean, I know you guys are having fun, and he's superhot, but how long can you continue seeing the guy who still wants to open a store that will become our biggest competitor?"

"I don't know. He hasn't said anything about Stone's New York. I know he's still looking at spaces, but nothing has been decided. Maybe nothing will come of it."

"I don't want to be the bearer of bad tidings, and

I'm not the person to dole out relationship advice, but in my experience, a man will always pick business first. Always. And with his family in the mix? It doesn't matter how much he likes you. He will eventually hurt you," Mindy said.

"That's the only reason we said anything to him last night," Sophie said. "We don't want you to get hurt."

Emma didn't have much of a stubborn streak, but she was certainly a willful person. She wasn't willing to give up on her and Daniel yet. She wanted to see if they could beat the odds. Find a way to make it work. "We're going away tomorrow morning. To Bermuda. For the weekend."

"When did this happen?" Mindy leaned forward and rested her elbows on her knees, seeming more than a little interested.

"Last night. After the pop-up. He said he wanted to get away from the spotlight and the businesses and spend some time together, just the two of us."

"Interesting." Mindy sat back, crossed her legs and bobbed her foot.

"What does that mean?" Emma asked.

Mindy shrugged. "It means it's interesting. Either he's being sweet or he's up to something."

"Like what?" Emma asked.

"Could be lots of things," Sophie said. "The history between our two families says that anything is possible."

Emma refused to believe she was going to end up being a cautionary tale. "I trust him. I'm not worried about it." That much was true, even when there was a voice in her head telling her that if Stone's New York happened, the odds were stacked against them. Could they truly ignore the rivalry between the stores? She didn't know the answer to that. It was like she and Daniel were inching forward in the dark, trying to find answers, while there were so many obstacles lurking in the shadows. She just had to believe in him. That was the only thing that made any sense. He wouldn't have asked her to get away with him if he didn't truly care about her.

"I need to get some work done." Mindy got up from her chair.

"Yeah, me, too." Emma followed her to the door.

"Hey, Emma," Sophie said. "I noticed that we still don't have the Nora Bradford agreement. We have to have it by the end of business today. I want to be able to walk into the office on Monday morning knowing that we have our most important designer signed for the next five years."

Emma swallowed hard, but held her head high like the entirely confident businesswoman she was still trying so hard to be. "Don't worry. You'll have it." She ducked out of Sophie's office and went in the opposite direction from Mindy, muttering to herself, "Even if I have to go over to Nora Bradford's office and camp out in the lobby all day long."

Hours later, Emma finally got the returned call she'd been waiting for. Nora Bradford's head of operations was on the phone.

"I'm so glad you called," Emma said, relief washing over her. "I don't know if there's a holdup in your legal department or what, but we still don't have the signed paperwork on the new licensing agreement. The old one expires on Monday and I think we'd all sleep a lot easier if we had everything in hand today. If we can get it done before five, I can arrange the first payment."

"Emma, I'm sorry, but we've had a change of direction. We aren't going to be signing the agreement."

"New direction? What in the world are you talking about? I thought this was a done deal."

"It was a done deal. But Nora got an offer from a different retailer a few days ago and it was just too good to pass up. They really rolled out the red carpet for us."

Emma was about to make a crack about how she had walked the red carpet for Nora Bradford, twice, but she felt like she was going to be sick. "Different retailer?"

"Yes. I'm afraid so. We're going to be working with Stone's."

Eleven

Emma couldn't believe the name she'd just heard. "I'm sorry. Did you say Stone's?"

"Yes. They're expanding into New York and the terms were too generous to pass up. Plus, it was probably time to make a change. Nora appreciates everything Eden's has done for her and we all loved your grandmother, but her passing was the end of an era."

An era I never knew. "Is there anything we can do to change your mind?"

"No. I'm sorry. I believe Stone's is making the announcement this afternoon. But please tell your sister that Nora is still willing to design her wedding dress."

"Oh. Okay." Like Sophie would want to wear a dress of betrayal on her wedding day. Emma hung up the phone, but she didn't have even a second to think before Sophie was yelling for her.

"Emma! Mindy! Get in here!"

Emma straightened her skirt, her mind a jumble of horrifying thoughts—the worst of which was that there was a very good chance her boyfriend had deceived her. She rushed into the hall. Mindy appeared, and they arrived at Sophie's door at the same time.

"What's going on?" Mindy asked.

Sophie held her finger to her lips and pointed at the flat screen TV on the wall, tuned to the twenty-four-hour business news channel. Mindy and Emma stepped inside and the three sisters stood shoulder to shoulder as the anchor, a woman who looked to be straight off the runway, spoke. "If you're just tuning in, we have major news in the retail world today. It appears that the rumors about Stone's department stores of London moving into New York are true. They seem poised to take down the legendary Eden's, which has been a fixture in Manhattan since the 1980s. They have also announced an exclusive licensing agreement with fashion designer Nora Bradford, known for her red carpet gowns and wedding dresses."

"Holy crap." Mindy pointed at the screen, then turned to Sophie and Emma. "What the hell, you two? I thought Nora Bradford was a done deal."

"I just got off the phone with them," Emma said. "I don't know what Stone's offered them, but it was enough to make them jump ship."

"When were you planning to tell us this?" Sophie's voice was so thin with distress it sounded like it might shatter.

"I told you. I just got off the phone with them."

"No. I mean when were you going to tell us that your boyfriend was screwing us over?"

Daniel. Everything she'd refused to believe was coming true. "I had no idea. He didn't say a thing. We tried very hard not to talk about business."

Sophie shook her head, tears streaming down her face. "Everything Gram worked so hard for. Down the tubes. It's all my fault. I'm CEO."

Emma didn't want to think about whose fault this really was. Had Daniel really betrayed her like this? She didn't want to believe it could be true. She pulled Sophie into a hug, and Mindy quickly had her arms around both of them. The three bowed their heads.

"We'll get through this," Mindy said. "We'll sign another designer even better than Nora. Or we'll start doing more private label clothing. Or both. Or we really ramp up our plans for the women's shoe department. There's always a pivot we can make. Always. And as for Stone's, maybe this is good. Maybe this is the kick in the butt we need."

The anchor was talking again, and the sisters watched. "Reporters spoke to Margaret Stone outside of her London home just minutes ago."

"Ms. Stone, what does this mean for your son's relationship with Emma Stewart, CFO of Eden's department store?" The reporter jammed the microphone in Daniel's mother's face.

Margaret Stone laughed as if Emma were a bug

on someone's shoe. "Daniel had his fun, but I knew it was over when he let me know last night that our lease was ready to sign. It was never going to last. She's an Eden, for God's sake."

"Have you talked to your son?"

She smiled. "I have. He couldn't be more pleased with today's developments."

Emma truly felt as though she'd been punched in the stomach. She staggered back until she had no choice but to plop down on the couch. She stared up at her sisters in utter disbelief. Everything they'd warned her of was coming true. She really was naive when it came to business, and apparently even more so when it came to love. "I don't know what to say. I'm just floored. By all of this. Am I an idiot for not wanting to believe that Daniel could do this?"

Mindy looked at her with the pity she'd come to hate so much. "No. Honey. You're not an idiot. But this is what we worried would happen. When we said we didn't want you to get hurt, we meant it."

Sophie sat on one side of Emma and Mindy sat on the other. "What are you going to do?" Sophie asked.

"I have to go talk to him. Right?"

"Yes. You have to confront him and take your chance to tell him to his face he's a jerk," Mindy said. "Otherwise you'll always regret it."

The thought of saying that to Daniel made it feel like her heart might crumble to dust. "So that's it, then."

Sophie patted her hand. "It'll be okay. I promise. You have Mindy and me. We're here for you. Even if it's the middle of the night and you need us to bring you ice cream."

"Or something stronger," Mindy added. "And Sophie's right. We have to stick together or we won't succeed. I don't think any of us has any interest in failing."

"So you don't blame me for this?" Emma asked.

Mindy stood and reached for Emma's hand to help her up. "We've all made mistakes that hurt Eden's. Especially me. We just need to know that Daniel Stone is done. No more trusting him. We know you like him, but that ship has sailed."

Emma walked to her office, numb. Seeing her desk and her office window brought to the forefront the memory of the pop-up night and all that had happened between them here. It had been more than passionate abandon. Daniel had seemed like he had such an incurable weakness for her. It had been an intoxicating thought. For the woman who'd worried whether she could be the kind who could turn Daniel Stone's head, she'd proved she not only could be, but that she was. And that had all happened after he knew the truth of her past. He didn't care that she'd come from nothing. He cared about the Emma of here and now.

Or so she had been foolish enough to think. She'd thought they could set aside business and bad blood between families. She should have been smart enough to realize those were the two things that drove Daniel and her the most. There was no compromise to be made, however badly she'd wanted to think there was.

She glanced at her phone and for an instant considered calling Daniel to tell him she was coming over. But no, he didn't deserve a heads-up. He deserved to be blindsided. Just as he'd done to her. She sent her driver a text, shut off her phone and rushed downstairs to go home.

Daniel stared at the television in disbelief. He would have missed this nightmare if a friend hadn't sent him a text congratulating him on signing the lease for Stone's New York. His mother. She just couldn't wait. She simply couldn't trust him. He watched as reporters caught up to her outside his family's London home. He cringed at her first answer, but the second truly made him want to retch. *He'd had his fun? It was never going to last?*

He had to get Emma on the phone right away, but he also needed to speak to his mother and get her to shut up and stop talking to the press. Every time she opened her mouth, she made it so much worse for him. As soon as Emma found out, she'd think the absolute worst of him. He sent her a text to buy himself ten or fifteen minutes.

I have some news I want you to hear from me. Can I come by your office?

He waited but got no response from Emma. His stomach rolled with the uncertainty. Did she already know? He didn't have time to worry further.

His mother answered the call without so much as a hello. "I guess you've seen the news."

Daniel wanted to scream. "What in bloody hell are you doing? You announce the lease before it's signed? You go to Nora Bradford behind my back?"

"You gave me no choice. You were never going to sign Nora. You were trying to curry favor with that woman you're seeing."

"Emma, Mother. Her name is Emma. And you don't know that to be true." Except that it was true. Emma was precisely the reason he'd tried to get out of enticing Nora Bradford to leave Eden's for Stone's. "This is a big problem for me. You've put me in a terrible situation. I can't talk about it now. I need to speak to Emma before she finds out what you did. But you and I need to have a conversation about my role in the company. I won't have you undermining me like this."

"We can talk about it on Monday after the lease is signed. How about dinner?"

"What?"

"I was thinking I should pop over for this momentous occasion."

"No. I do not need your supervision. I have everything in hand."

"So you don't want to see me?"

Daniel grumbled over the phone. How she loved to lay on the maternal guilt. "I'm only saying that you don't need to make the trip. It seems silly."

"Okay, well, I'll be there, silly or not. I want to see you and the new store. I know you're upset, but you'll see that this was everything we needed to do.

You'll meet another woman. There are always more women."

Not like Emma. Daniel heard a knock at his door. The dogs ran right over and started barking. "I have to go." He ended the call and tossed his phone onto the table, rushing for the door. "Enough. Sit," he said to the dogs, which immediately piped down and followed instructions. Even Jolly.

Daniel opened the door. The sight of Emma nearly mowed him over. She was breathtaking beautiful, but there were ragged edges to her now. She knew what had happened. He could see it on her face. He felt the disappointment radiating off her. "Please. Come in. I tried to reach you."

"You did?" The dogs were begging for her attention, and Emma crouched down to pet them all.

"I sent you a text."

"I didn't get it. I turned off my phone after I saw the atrocity on TV. What in the hell happened, Daniel? Have you been lying to me this whole time?" She stood and smoothed her hair back, a deep crease forming between her eyes.

"No. Of course not. The Nora Bradford thing was my mother's doing."

"But did you know she was pursuing her?"

He couldn't lie. He couldn't hide anything else from her. "I did."

Her shoulders dropped in disappointment. "How long? How long have you known?"

"Since before I met you. I was sent to talk to her that night at Empire State. But we hardly knew each other then, and I knew you were tied to Eden's. I couldn't say anything. Plus, it was just an idea then." He reached for her, but she turned away. The disappointment that registered in his body was so deep it went down to the soles of his feet.

"An idea to hurt Eden's."

"Yes. My mother's idea, mind you. Not mine."

"Does it really matter? The net effect is the same. This is a huge hit for our store. Sophie and Mindy are so upset."

"Please tell me they aren't angry with you. I'll talk to them if you need me to. I'll tell them you knew nothing about it."

"Actually, they're being nothing but supportive. They resisted the temptation to remind me that they'd told me exactly what you were going to do. They told me you would ultimately betray me and I didn't believe them. That's how stupid I am."

Daniel ran his hands through his hair. "I didn't betray you, Emma. I swear I didn't know about actually signing Nora Bradford, and my plan was to tell you about the lease this weekend during our trip."

"So you were planning to sweep me off my feet with your private plane and your getaway, just so you could tell me that I'd better prepare myself for the fight of my life? How did you think that was going to go over, exactly? Did you think I was going to congratulate you? Be excited?"

He drew in a deep breath. He'd really done a horrible job of thinking this through. "I guess I hoped you might handle it like every other conflicted moment we've had together. I hoped that you'd decide that you liked me more than you hated my business."

"This is more than your business. It's your family, too. You stand by them, and I have no choice but to do the same with mine."

He refused to believe that this had to be an impasse. They had to find some way through this. "So you'd rather be loyal to Sophie and Mindy than me? Even after everything the Eden family has done to you? For your entire life?"

"What choice do I have? These are ties that I don't want broken. They're ties I've wanted my entire life. Plus, you cannot preach to me about family loyalty. I know that comes first for you. Even after your mother has treated you terribly. Even after your brother betrayed you. You cling to the Stone name exactly like I'm clinging to my own."

"I don't want to cling to my name if it means I'm going to lose you."

"I heard what your mother said about me. Do you think there's ever any coming back from that? If I'm going to be with a man, I need his family to accept me. To welcome me. I've spent my entire life feeling lost. Searching for the place where I would belong. I'm not going back to that. We would never overcome it."

"What are you saying, Emma?" He held his breath. It would mean moving forward, and he didn't want to do that without her. He didn't just sense that his heart was about to break, he felt it.

Tears were streaming down her face. "I'm saying

that there's no future for us, Daniel. And if there's no future, we're done. I can't merely have fun with you. I can't sleep with you and pretend like it doesn't mean something. Aside from maybe that first night at Empire State, I don't think we were ever only having fun. There has always been a serious undercurrent between us."

"That's part of what I loved so much. We fell into sync. So quickly."

"And that's what makes this ridiculously hard." She looked down at her hands as she wrung them together. When she looked back up at him with those warm brown eyes he adored, he knew she was about to deliver a crushing blow. "Because the truth is that I love you. I know it sounds silly, but it's the truth. I've had those words waiting on my lips many times and I never had the nerve to say them."

Everything in his body went impossibly still. "So you're saying them now?"

"I don't want to regret this any more than I already do. Our cards should all be out on the table. Let's leave nothing unsaid."

Daniel swallowed back the emotion of the moment. He dreaded telling her his true feelings, only because he knew she no longer cared to return them.

"Goodbye, Daniel. I really do wish you the best." She kissed him on the cheek and reached for the door. "But you should know that my sisters and I are committed to kicking your family's ass."

Twelve

After a weekend without Emma, Daniel's greatest fear was that the emptiness would be permanent this time. At least it was familiar. He'd felt exactly like this after William died and Bea left. His father had given himself over to the despair, while his mother defied it, tightening her chokehold on the family business and Daniel. Meanwhile, loneliness, guilt and doubt brewed a toxic cocktail in Daniel's head.

He hadn't been doing that much better when he arrived in New York, but at least he had a charge to distract him—opening Stone's New York. This morning, he'd get back on course and sign the lease. The trouble was, his heart didn't want to go there. His heart was too hung up on Emma.

He rolled over in bed and that made the dogs stir.

He waited for a growl from Jolly, but it never came. Instead, she crept toward him until her nose nudged his hand for a pet. He pulled her nearer and ruffled her ears. This one remaining piece of his brother's life was so special to him, but it had taken Emma to bring them closer. That was what she did—she made everything and everyone around her better.

She'd helped him see the joy and beauty around him, perhaps because she'd spent so much of her life going without. She'd shaken him awake, turned him from a man who ignored a stranger's conversation in the elevator to someone who could face things he'd been avoiding for years, like the press. She showed him that the world wasn't a dismal place. It could be so beautiful, especially with her in it.

His chest ached just thinking about her. Although his longing was so much more than physical, it manifested itself as pain. Chronic agony. Whoever said that love hurts had been absolutely right. He'd thought he'd loved Bea, but he hadn't. Not like this. What he had with Emma was once-in-a-lifetime. Irreplaceable. If he had any chance at all of living a happy life, he had to get her back. But he didn't see how that was possible. Not with their families standing between them.

He glanced at the clock. The signing had been moved to ten o'clock by the property manager, so he had only a little more than two hours. His mother was due to land at the private airstrip at JFK in an hour. Charlotte would be on hand to sign the paperwork. He'd worked to reach this milestone. He'd wanted it.

But he couldn't help but think that his name on that dotted line would be like signing the final death decree of his romance with Emma. She would never take him back then. Perhaps it was best to get it over with. He had to pick himself up and move forward. Somehow.

He slogged through his normal morning routine of tea and walking the dogs. He didn't stop by the newsstand. He was done with that. He couldn't stomach the thought of showing up and seeing Emma splashed across the front page. No matter what they said about her, good or bad, it would hurt like hell. He followed it up with a shower, but skipped the shave. His mother despised his five o'clock shadow. If he had to be unhappy, she might as well be, too.

He dreaded having to take her to task at dinner this evening, but it had to be done. It wasn't merely to make his professional life better. She needed help. He was certain she still hadn't truly mourned William's death. He needed to help her see that it was time to stop. And take a breath. At the very least, she needed to loosen the reins and give him full autonomy in New York. And once he returned to London, they needed to devise her exit plan from the company. If she wasn't willing to do that, he wasn't sure what he'd do. Quitting would mean walking away from his family. He didn't have that in him, however miserable he was.

Daniel's driver met him in the parking garage and got him to the store in record time. He looked out the window for a glimpse of their new building, but as they approached, he saw that his worst nightmare was waiting for him—the press. Photographers. All of them waiting outside.

"Is there another entrance?" he asked.

"Aside from the loading dock, I don't think so. It's probably not open, anyway, since the building is empty."

Daniel pressed his lips together. He'd do this. He'd live. "Okay. Thanks. I've got my door." He jumped out and straightened his suit coat. "Morning," he said, marching forward while people shoved cameras in his face and shouted questions at him. He didn't stop, didn't want to look, and certainly didn't want to listen. They were asking about Emma and it nearly killed him.

He rushed through the glass doors into the grand and empty space. Charlotte was waiting for him, along with the representative from the property company.

"Hello, Charlotte," Daniel said. "Thanks for taking care of this."

"My pleasure." She shook his hand and introduced him to the landlord. "Everything look good?" she asked Daniel.

He turned and surveyed the sprawling main floor. It was just as amazing as he'd remembered it, Carrara marble everywhere—floors, arches and pillars. Vintage art deco chandeliers hung from the twenty-foot ceilings. There were very few spaces like this in New York anymore. He was lucky to have found it, but he didn't feel that way. "Yes. Let's hope my mother agrees."

"It looks as though she's just arrived," Charlotte said, nodding toward the entrance.

Daniel turned and watched as his mother climbed out of her stretch limo. She was wearing a pale blue Chanel suit, black pumps and oversize sunglasses. Her light brown hair was in a perfect bob, not a strand out of place. She immediately walked up to the members of the press who had gathered, took off her sunglasses and began regaling them with some sort of tale. He had no idea what she was saying, but they were laughing while they snapped their pictures. The next thing he knew, she was waving them all in.

"In we go, everyone. Take as many pictures as you like. Of course, it'll look quite different once my son and I have gotten our hands on it." She made her way over to Daniel. "Hello, darling. How are you?" They kissed on both cheeks. "You look skinny."

Of course he did. He'd been too distracted by Emma to ever think about food, and since losing her, he'd had no appetite. "Nice to see you."

She tapped her sunglasses against her chin as she looked high and low, getting her first full view of the new store. "The space is wonderful. I love it."

Daniel was relieved about that much. He'd gotten this one thing right.

One of the photographers stepped toward them. "Mr. Stone. Ms. Stone. Can you turn around for some pictures?"

"Why didn't you tell me you were inviting the

media?" he asked out of the side of his mouth. "Shouldn't we wait for those favors when the store actually opens?"

"Because all publicity is good and you're a hot property right now." She spoke through her perfect smile as they posed.

"No I'm not. And I don't like the idea of being paraded around."

"Daniel? Is it over between you and Emma Stewart?" one of the reporters asked.

His heart sank at the mere mention of her name. "I'm not discussing that today."

The photographers finished taking pictures of them and returned their attention to the store. In one corner, a camera crew was setting up.

"Smart of you not to answer the question," his mother said. "I think it's probably best if we ignore the question of the Eden girl and pretend like it never happened."

"Daniel? Are we ready to sign?" Charlotte asked.

"Yes. Indeed," his mother answered. She strolled over to the small table where the paperwork was set out.

Daniel didn't move. His feet simply wouldn't go. He didn't want to ignore anything about Emma. He didn't want to pretend like it had never happened. He'd been happy with her and he wasn't willing to let go of that.

"Daniel. Come on," his mother said. "We'll sign it together."

He managed to pick up his feet, but every step felt

wrong. Putting his name on those papers might put a solid wall of concrete between Emma and him, but not signing wouldn't mend his heart. He'd still be the sad and empty version of himself, and he didn't want to be that man anymore. He wanted to be his best self and he was that only with Emma.

He walked up to his mother and Charlotte. "I'm not signing." His words echoed in his head, but they felt right. It felt good to get them out of the way.

"Don't be silly," his mother said.

"Is something wrong?" Charlotte asked.

"I need a moment with my mother, if that's alright." The press in the room had figured out that something was amiss and were closing in, just like they loved to do. "And I need you all to back off," he said to them sternly. "Please."

"You're embarrassing me." His mother's jaw was firmly set.

"I'm sorry. Truly. I am. But this was never the right thing to do. I wanted this for you because you wanted it. I thought it might make you happy. But I can't see this through because it all started out of hatred."

"It's business. Nothing else."

He shook his head. "No. I'm not buying that. It's more than that and you know it. You want to show the world that you're invincible and that we won't let the bad things knock us down. But this is a distraction from the real work that needs to be done. You and I and Dad are never going to get past William's death until we stop worrying over the family business and get back to the business of being a family."

"You're my son and my employee, and I expect this of you."

"You're my mother and I expect you to want me to be happy." There would be hell to pay for what he was about to say, but hopefully, she'd one day see that this was all for love. A love that could not be bought, or negotiated, or replaced. There was only one way out of this. "I'm not signing. I'm quitting. Effective immediately."

Mondays were never Emma's favorite day of the workweek, but today was especially bad and she'd been in the office for only two hours. It was going to be a long day. Being at Eden's was like attending a funeral. There was an overriding sense of doom, a dark cloud overhead. She felt responsible. She'd let Daniel into their world, even when everyone told her to keep him out. She'd been naive and stupid. She'd been everything she'd never wanted to be. Princess Emma was a fool.

Mindy appeared at her door with a newspaper in hand. "Got a minute?"

"Whatever you're about to tell me, whatever's in that thing, I don't want to hear it. Especially if it has anything to do with Stone's or Daniel." Her voice cracked. It might be a while before she'd ever be able to say his name again without wanting to cry.

Mindy walked right in and dropped the paper on Emma's desk. "Pratt Institute. Student fashion show. We should go. Maybe we can get in on the ground floor with some promising new designers."

"Look at you. Actually wanting the store to be successful."

She shrugged. "I work best when everything is falling apart. I have no idea why."

Emma skimmed the story while Mindy sat in an available chair. "Friday?"

"Unless you have other plans."

Emma twisted her lips into an unhappy bundle. "You know I don't have plans. I have no life outside of work. Just like before."

"Precisely. We're two peas in a pod. We could go out for a drink afterward. Flirt with handsome men. It'll be fun."

Emma blew out a breath through her nose. "The first part sounds okay. I don't need to go out and flirt with anyone. I'm done with men."

"Too soon, huh?"

"Yes. And you've only been broken up from Sam for a few days yourself. Are you really ready to start meeting people?"

"It's easier when it's the third or fourth time you've broken up." She tucked her hair behind her ears. "But no, I'm not really ready. I like to tell myself I'm ready. I'm not."

"Okay. Good. I was starting to worry that I might be acting like a wimp."

"You aren't. I get it." Mindy got up from her chair. "So Friday? Do we have a date?"

"Can I get back to you? I might not be up to it."

Mindy waved her closer. "Come here. Give me a hug."

For a moment, Emma wondered if she was in a parallel universe where Mindy was the caring, sensitive one. Still, she gladly took the embrace from her sister. The trouble was, the instant she was in Mindy's arms, tears began to roll down her cheeks.

Mindy smoothed Emma's hair and rocked her back and forth. "Everything will be okay. I promise. I know you were head over heels for him, but I promise you there will be other guys."

She couldn't imagine any man ever matching up to Daniel. He made her a stronger version of herself. She'd felt invincible with him. Probably why she'd been so convinced that their obstacles didn't have to be a problem. "I don't want another guy."

"The cards were stacked against you two. Sometimes things happen that way. Too much family history. Too much money and business in the mix."

"Yeah. You're right." Emma took in a deep breath, but she still wasn't convinced. Hopefully, time would help her get there.

"You want to grab lunch?"

Emma stood back and shook her head. "No. I think I'm going to run back to my apartment and eat something there. I need some quiet." What she really needed was time away from Eden's, if only for a few hours.

"Okay. I'll see you later this afternoon."

Gregory drove Emma back to her building. She hoped that eventually it would again feel like coming home. Right now, it felt like a trap. She was terrified of running into Daniel. She didn't want to fall apart. She wanted to be whole again.

"Ms. Stewart," Henry the doorman said. "I'm wondering if you can give me Mr. Stone's mobile number. He forgot to give it to me and his dog walker hasn't shown up."

"And he's not home?"

Henry shook his head. "He won't be back until later this afternoon."

Emma dug her phone out of her purse but thought twice about it. It was silly, but she hadn't had a chance to say goodbye to the dogs, and she loved them. "I have a key. I'll walk the dogs."

"You sure?"

She nodded and smiled. "Yep."

Upstairs, the dogs started to bark as soon as she put the key in the door. She scrambled inside and they ran around her, circling her legs and jumping "Shh. Shh." She crouched down and showed all three some love. She was going to miss them. At least Daniel had some company. He needed that, all alone in the city.

She went to get the leashes from the hook but was drawn to step into the living room. She loved his place, possibly more than her own. It smelled like him. It felt like him. It was warm and cozy and made her feel secure and comfortable. Just seeing his sofa brought back memories of watching movies and laughing and not making it to the end before clothes started coming off. They'd been so consumed by each other that the outside world had mattered very little to her. That had been her solution for moving forward with Daniel—keep everyone and everything else out. But the forces of the outside world had crept back in.

She couldn't stay in his apartment any longer. It simply hurt too much. She hooked up the dogs and got them downstairs and across the street. The sky was clouding over and rain was threatening, so she quickly started on the shortest of Daniel's routes, the dogs leading the way. Even the park no longer held the allure it once had. It would always make her think of him—their first real kiss, the moments of getting to know each other, the instances when she'd felt like he might be the only thing she ever needed. Of course, that wasn't true. That wasn't reality. She needed her family. Her sisters.

A raindrop fell on her nose. And another. She looked up, to find gray storm clouds swirling. "Come on, guys, we need to get going." They walked double time as the rain began to fall softly.

"Emma!" The voice was somewhere behind her. The press had tracked her down in the park. This was the last thing she wanted to deal with. She started to run, but between her heels and Jolly's little legs, she could go only so fast.

"Emma! Stop! Please!"

She ground to a halt, the dogs just as surprised as she was, looking back at her. She turned around and there was a vision she'd feared she'd never see. Daniel was running toward her. She stood frozen until the dogs took off in his direction, Emma following along, clutching their leashes.

She and Daniel were both out of breath when they

got to each other. The rain was coming down hard, but it was warm, and he was such a heavenly sight it made her heart flutter.

"Your dog walker didn't show up," she said. "I didn't want them to destroy your apartment."

"I know. Henry told me. That's why I came looking for you. We need to talk."

She fought back the optimism that wanted to walk through the door he'd just opened. "Is there anything left to say? I don't want us to torture each other."

"I quit my job."

She blinked back the rain that was starting to roll down her forehead. "You what?"

"I quit my job. I refused to sign the lease. I couldn't do it. I couldn't hurt you like that."

Thunder clapped overhead. "We need to get out of the rain. You'll ruin your suit."

He shook his head and took her hand. "You think I care about this thing? I don't. I only care about you. I'm not going anywhere until you tell me what you're thinking."

Her heart was heavy right now. She appreciated his sacrifice, but it wasn't right. "I don't want you to give up your family because of me, Daniel. That's not what I wanted."

The raindrops had weighed his hair down in the front. He dragged it back with his fingers. "I didn't give up my family. I gave up my job so I could do a better job of being *in* my family. It wasn't working. I need to be a son, not an employee."

She took his hand and led him under a tree to

shield them from the rain. She was still struggling to understand what he'd done. "You did all of this to apologize?"

He didn't let go of her fingers, just held on tighter. "Apologize. Make amends. Turn over a new leaf. I don't want to go another minute without you, Emma. I don't think I can move forward until we see where this goes." He swallowed so hard she could see his Adam's apple bob up and down. His face was dotted with raindrops. His suit was drenched. "I love you, Emma. I think I loved you from the minute you walked up to me and made me laugh."

Her heart was now flying circles in her chest, but she had to know one thing. "I told you I loved you the other day and you didn't say it back."

"I know. I was stupid. The words were there, but I wasn't thinking straight. But I realized this morning that the most important thing to me has always been loyalty. And loyalty is so much more than an act. You have to have it in your heart." He stepped closer and set his fingers on Emma's chest, right at the base of her throat. "You have the most loyal and generous heart I have ever known. I need you in my life. Will you take me back? Will you give me another chance?"

Emma scanned his handsome face, her heart pounding. What was she waiting for? He was everything she'd ever wanted, everything she'd once only dared to wish for. "You were brave enough to tear down the wall between us. I want nothing more than another chance. I love you. That's not going anywhere."

"Good. Because I'm not going anywhere, either."

"What about London?"

He smiled and tugged her closer. "What about it? I can visit it anytime. But for now, as long as I have you, my home is in New York."

All she could do was wonder if this was real. The only thing that was putting her in the present was the rain and his eyes. They told her that Mindy was right. Everything would be okay. It had to be. She'd come too far for it not to be. "I thought you didn't really like it here."

"I know I said that, but I met the most incredible woman and she makes me see things in a whole new way."

"She sounds awesome." Emma smiled.

"She's better than awesome. She's a princess." He gathered her into his arms, and Emma pressed herself hard against the solid plane of his body. She kissed him without hesitation and he did the same. There was no more wall between them. He'd torn it down. This was their new beginning. Even in the rain, his warmth poured into her, or maybe that was love that made her feel so wholly content, from head to toe.

"Can we go inside now?" she asked.

"I thought you'd never ask. I'm dying to get you out of those wet clothes."

Epilogue

Emma looked out the airplane window at the stretch of pale sky and wispy clouds. Far below was the deep cobalt churn of the Atlantic. "How much longer until we get there?"

Daniel finished off his glass of champagne and shook his wrist to consult his watch. "An hour? We should be starting our descent soon."

He took her hand and she looked down at their entwined fingers. Her heart was galloping just like it did every time she started to think about what was waiting for them when they landed—Daniel's mother and father. He wanted the unthinkable to happen. He wanted Emma to spend time with his family.

He'd only recently started speaking to his mother again. He'd let her cool off for a good two months after quitting his job. But now that she had unofficially halted any plans for Stone's New York, he wanted to begin the process of mending fences, and that apparently meant pulling Emma into the family fold. Hence the trip to London. On the family's private jet, no less. She hoped that was a sign they might accept her. It seemed doubtful you'd send a plane for someone you didn't like, although Emma was still getting used to the funny things rich people did. Even though she was one herself.

"What if they don't like me? What if your mother kicks me out of the house?" She'd asked him these questions several times over the last week or so, but once more didn't seem excessive.

"We've been through this. You'll win her over."

"I hope so. It means a lot to me to have her approval." Emma didn't want to pin too much on this trip, but it was another test. There was no doubt about that.

"If you don't, it doesn't matter. I love you and I approve of you and that's all that matters."

"If you say so." She sucked in a deep breath, reminding herself that everything he said was true. "She's going to ask about Eden's, isn't she? Should I tell her we aren't doing well? That the store is teetering on the brink?" The loss of Nora Bradford had been a big one. Sophie was worried, but she was also focused on her wedding. Mindy was strategizing, while trying her hardest to stay away from Sam. Emma was busy keeping things moving forward, and she wanted to do exactly that with Daniel.

"You tell her the store is doing great and you change the subject."

"She's going to ask about the menswear line." This was Daniel's new venture. He'd curated everything in the men's department at Stone's over the last several years. That was part of the reason it was their most successful department. "She's going to want to know where you plan to sell it."

"And I'll tell her I don't know yet. Plus, this is a test run for me. It might flop."

As if anything Daniel ever did could be considered a failure. "Or it might be a huge success."

"One can only hope. If not, I'll look into something else. I have plenty of ideas up here." He tapped his temple.

Emma leaned over the center armrest and kissed him softly. "Such a handsome place to keep ideas."

He smiled, his eyes half-closed. "I try."

Sometimes when she looked at him, she needed someone to pinch her. Being with him was still so much like living in a dream. "Do you think she feels like you're trying to push her?"

"If she does, it's only because I am. I never imagined that quitting would finally get her to truly pay attention to what I want, but it has."

Daniel had double-downed on his love for Emma when he'd left his family's company. He'd been the one who made the big sacrifice. Yes, his job had been making him crazy, but she knew very well that it hadn't been easy for him to walk away, even though he tried to make it seem as if it had been the only logical course of action. He could have taken the situation in any number of directions, but he'd chosen the one that led back to her, and she couldn't be any more thankful.

But it bothered her that she hadn't found a way to make a similar overture. A grand gesture. Yes, she'd moved into his apartment, but that was only because the dogs were more comfortable there and he had an even better view. Otherwise, she'd had to do very little other than love him, which was impossibly simple. It was so easy it was like breathing.

"Daniel?"

"Yes?"

"Do you believe in fate?" Emma had wondered a lot about this over the last few weeks while she'd been mulling a way to show Daniel just how much she loved and adored him. She had a question tumbling around in her head, but she worried how he would react. They'd been together for only three months. Plus, there were certainly things about Daniel that were old-fashioned, or at the very least steeped in tradition. She didn't want to push him too far outside his comfort zone. He'd been pushed around plenty.

He sat back in his seat, seeming deeply contemplative. "I never really thought about it. I mean, I know now what it feels like to be with the right person, and it does seem like awfully good luck that we met, but there was some other force at work when you walked up to me at Empire State and struck up a conversation. Especially considering that I'd been a complete ass to you the day before."

Good. That was exactly what she thought. Hello, same wavelength. "So we set these things in motion. We have to take steps to get what we want."

"Yes. Exactly. I don't want to live in a world where I don't have some say in what happens."

She had a great deal of what she wanted—a job she loved and two sisters she grew closer to every day. There had been a time in the not-so-distant past when none of this would have seemed possible. She didn't want to be greedy, but she wanted it all. She didn't feel like waiting to make it happen.

Emma scooted forward in her seat and looked at Daniel. "You know I love you, right?"

He cocked his head to one side, his eyes narrowing. "Yes. Of course. I love you, too. Why do you ask?"

She took both his hands and pulled them into her lap. "I just want you to really know. I don't ever want you to question it."

"Please don't tell me you're dying of an incurable disease."

"What? No."

He breathed a sigh of relief. "Good. I was starting to wonder."

"I just need you to know that you're the only person I want to be with. And I felt like I needed to say this before we landed in London. Before we went to see your parents. Because I know we've already had two beginnings, but it feels like right now is another one." She scanned his face, still awfully nice to look at when he was so confused. "I want you to marry me, Daniel. It doesn't have to be tomorrow or next week or even next year. But someday. I want you to know that I don't want anyone else. You're all I'll ever want or need." Emma was so proud of getting out the words, even if she'd rambled.

"Emma." His shoulders dropped and her stomach felt like it went right with them. "What in the world am I going to do with you?"

"Are you mad?"

He looked...well, he didn't look happy. In fact, he unbuckled his seat belt and got up, stepping across the aisle to where he'd left his carry-on bag. He unzipped a side pocket, took his seat again and placed an ivory-colored velvet box on the armrest between them.

"What's this?"

"Open it." He underscored his invitation with a pop of his eyebrows.

She did as he asked, and inside the box was a ring that knocked the wind right out of her—a glimmering oval, icy-blue gemstone surrounded by diamonds. It was the same color as the dress she'd worn for Empire State. "Aquamarine?"

He nodded. "It is."

"It's beautiful. I don't even know what to say."

"This is my side of the question you asked."

She was both elated and feeling guilty. "Did I ruin your proposal?"

"It definitely didn't go according to plan, but that's okay. I hadn't worked out exactly when I was going to ask. I was mostly bringing it as insurance. If my mother got too horrible, I was hoping I could convince you to stay with a ring."

Emma dropped her head to one side as Daniel took the ring from the box and slipped it on her hand. She waggled her fingers. "It's beautiful. I love it." She pried her eyes away to look at him. "More than anything, I love that we were thinking the same thing."

"Full confession, I've been thinking about this for a while. I bought it before we broke up."

"You did?"

"Yes. Shows you how desperate I was to find a way to keep you. But you know, I'm glad it happened this way. We did this together, just like we're going to do so many other things together." He leaned closer. "Now come here and kiss me."

His lips settled on hers and her eyes fluttered shut. Kissing Daniel was the best, mostly because she always felt reassured that he loved her. And she could show him how much she returned the sentiment.

"What's your mother going to say?"

"Honestly, this might be a brilliant stroke of luck on our part. How can she hold a grudge against an Eden who's about to become a Stone?"

* * * * *

Get 4 FREE REWARDS!

We'll send you 2 FREE Books plus 2 FREE Mystery Gifts.

Harlequin® Desire books feature heroes who have it all: wealth, status, incredible good looks... everything but the right woman.

FREE Value Over $20

YES! Please send me 2 FREE Harlequin® Desire novels and my 2 FREE gifts (gifts are worth about $10 retail). After receiving them, if I don't wish to receive any more books, I can return the shipping statement marked "cancel." If I don't cancel, I will receive 6 brand-new novels every month and be billed just $4.55 per book in the U.S. or $5.24 per book in Canada. That's a savings of at least 13% off the cover price! It's quite a bargain! Shipping and handling is just 50¢ per book in the U.S. and $1.25 per book in Canada.* I understand that accepting the 2 free books and gifts places me under no obligation to buy anything. I can always return a shipment and cancel at any time. The free books and gifts are mine to keep no matter what I decide.

225/326 HDN GNND

Name (please print)	
Address	Apt. #
City	State/Province	Zip/Postal Code

Mail to the **Reader Service:**
IN U.S.A.: P.O. Box 1341, Buffalo, NY 14240-8531
IN CANADA: P.O. Box 603, Fort Erie, Ontario L2A 5X3

Want to try 2 free books from another series? Call 1-800-873-8635 or visit www.ReaderService.com.

SPECIAL EXCERPT FROM

HQN™

Gabe Dalton knows he should ignore his attraction to Jamie Dodge…but her tough-talking attitude masks an innocence that tempts him past breaking point…

Read on for a sneak preview of
Cowboy to the Core
by New York Times *and* USA TODAY
bestselling author Maisey Yates.

"You sure like coming up to me guns blazing, Jamie Dodge. Just saying whatever it is that's on your mind. No concern for the fallout of it. Well, all things considered, I'm pretty sick of keeping myself on a leash."

He cupped her face, and in the dim light he could see that she was staring up at him, her eyes wide. And then, without letting another breath go by, he dipped his head and his lips crushed up against Jamie Dodge's.

They were soft.

Good God, she was soft.

He didn't know what he had expected.

Prickles, maybe.

But no, her lips were the softest, sweetest thing he'd felt in a long time. It was like a flash of light had gone off and erased everything in his brain, like all his thoughts had been printed on an old-school film roll.

There was nothing.

Nothing beyond the sensation of her skin beneath his fingertips, the feel of her mouth under his. She was frozen beneath his touch, and he shifted, tilting his head to the side and darting his tongue out, flicking it against the seam of her lips.

PHMYEXP0719

She gasped, and he took advantage of that, getting entry into that pretty mouth so he could taste her, deep and long, and exactly how he'd been fantasizing about.

Oh, those fantasies hadn't been a fully realized scroll of images. No. It had been a feeling.

An invisible band of tension that had stretched between them in small spaces of time. In the leap of panic in his heart when he'd seen her fall from the horse earlier today.

It had been embedded in all of those things and he hadn't realized exactly what it meant he wanted until the right moment. And then suddenly it was like her shock transformed into something else entirely.

She arched toward him, her breasts pressing against his chest, her hands coming up to his face. She thrust her chin upward, making the kiss harder, deeper. He drove his tongue deep, sliding it against hers, and she made a small sound like a whimpering kitten. The smallest sound he'd ever heard Jamie Dodge make.

He pulled away from her, nipped her lower lip and then pressed his mouth to hers one more time before releasing his hold.

She looked dazed. He felt about how she looked.

"I thought about it," he said. "And I realized I couldn't let this one go. I let you criticize my riding, question my authority, but I wasn't about to let you get away with cock-blocking me, telling me you're jealous and then telling me you don't know if you want me. So I figured maybe I'd give you something to think about."

Don't miss
Cowboy to the Core *by Maisey Yates,*
available July 2019 wherever
Harlequin® *books and ebooks are sold.*

www.Harlequin.com

PHMYEXP0719

*Dealing with her insufferable hotshot boss has
India Crowley at the breaking point. But when he faces
a stand-in daddy dilemma, India can't deny him a
helping hand. Sharing close quarters, though,
may mean facing her true feelings about the man...*

Read on for a sneak peek at
BIG SHOT
by New York Times *bestselling author Katy Evans!*

I hate my boss

My demanding, stone-hearted, arrogant bastard boss.

You know those people in an elevator who click the close button repeatedly when they see someone coming just to avoid human contact? You know what?

That's my boss. But worse.

As I settle in, I notice that my boss, William, isn't around.

He's the kind of person who turns up early to work for no good reason. It's probably because he has no social life—he's a lone wolf, according to my mother, but to me, that translates as he's a jerk with no friends. Despite the lackeys who follow him around everywhere, I know he doesn't have any real friends. After all, I control his calendar for personal appointments, and in truth, there aren't many.

But where is he today? Not being early is like being late for him. Until he arrives, there's little I can do, so I meander to the coffee machine and make a cup for myself. As the machine is churning up coffee beans, the elevator dings and William appears.

I'll admit, something about his presence always knocks the breath from me. He stalks forward, with three people following in his wake. His hair is perfectly slicked, his stubble trimmed close to his sharp jaw. His eyes are a shocking blue. I can picture him now on the front cover of *Business Insider*, his piercing eyes radiating confidence from the page. But today his eyes are clouded by anger.

He spots me waiting. The whole office is watching as he stalks toward me with a bunch of papers in his arms. His colleagues struggle to keep up, and I discard my coffee, suddenly fearful of his glare. Did I do something wrong?

"Good morning, Mr. Walker—"

"Good morning, India," he growls.

He shoves the papers into my arms and I almost topple over in surprise. "I need you to sort out this paperwork mess and I don't want to hear another word from you until it's done." When he stalks away without so much as a smile, I notice I've been holding my breath.

And this is why, despite his beauty, despite his money, despite his drive, I can't stand the man.

Will she feel the same way when
they're in close quarters? Find out in
BIG SHOT
by New York Times *bestselling author Katy Evans.*

Available August 2019 wherever
Harlequin® Desire books and ebooks are sold.

www.Harlequin.com